Midnight Masquerade

By

Ellen Dugan

ACKNOWLEDGMENTS

Thanks to my friends Terry, Necole, John Philip, Shawna,
Michelle, and Mickie who listened while I debated over how
Gabriella's story would turn out. Ends up that yes, a dark horse
character *was* the way to go with this tale.

Thanks as always to my beta readers, and to Mitchell for the
editing and formatting.

Finally, this book is dedicated to my husband, Ken. Our life may
not be a romance novel, but after thirty-six years and counting...it's
still my favorite love story.

Other titles by Ellen Dugan

THE LEGACY OF MAGICK SERIES

Legacy Of Magick, Book 1

Secret Of The Rose, Book 2

Message Of The Crow, Book 3

Beneath An Ivy Moon, Book 4

Under The Holly Moon, Book 5

The Hidden Legacy, Book 6

Spells Of The Heart, Book 7

Sugarplums, Spells & Silver Bells, Book 8

Magick & Magnolias, Book 9 (Coming 2018)

Mistletoe & Ivy, Book 10 (Coming 2019)

THE GYPSY CHRONICLES

Gypsy At Heart, Book 1

Tear off the mask.
Your face is glorious.

-Rumi

CHAPTER ONE

I'd made up my mind.

I was going to tell Max Dubois how I felt about him. I'd waited for the perfect occasion and a romantic opportunity had at last presented itself. I, Gabriella Midnight, mild mannered graphic designer, the quiet and dependable middle sister of the daughters of Midnight, was *finally* going to go and get her man.

The party for the *Trois Amis* Winery's grand opening was only a few days away, and I was frantically trying to find something amazing to wear. After all, if I was going to sweep a man off his feet, I needed to set the stage for seduction...so to speak.

Now, I was scouting the shops with my younger sister, hoping that I might stumble

Ellen Dugan

across a dress I could turn into something worthy of a fancy masquerade party. I'd procrastinated, as usual, and had put off going dress shopping until the last minute. As I worked my way through the evening gowns on a sales rack, I felt a touch of panic over the lack of worthy options.

*Nope. No. Dear god no...*With a cringe I thought about all of the gorgeous romance novel covers I'd designed in the past few years and wondered why *I* wasn't finding an evening gown that captured my imagination. I needed an amazing sale price and a bit of magick if I hoped to pull off wooing the man of my dreams. I frowned over a sequined red slip dress, dismissed it as too Jessica Rabbit, and wondered if it was possible to find anything worthy of an enchanted evening.

"Ella!" my sister Cammy called to me.

I swung my head around and discovered she was waving me over. I put the red number back on the rack.

"I found some prom dresses on sale!" Cammy said, excitedly.

I balked. "Prom dresses?" I frowned at her.

"I'm twenty-seven years old. I'm not wearing a prom dress."

"Prom dress, bridesmaid dress, evening gown, what does it matter? Between the two of us, we can find something and make it work," Cammy said from over the mound of taffeta and tulle that was bundled in her arms. She pointed me toward a dressing room. "Let's try these on."

I was stuffed in a dressing room before I could blink. My sister, shy retiring thing that she was, came right in with me. I sighed. "Jeez, Cammy."

"What?" She raised a single brow. "I think I may found something I can use too."

Rolling my eyes to the ceiling, I peeled off my clothes and began trying on dresses. The first one was hot pink in shimmery taffeta. The dress was slim fitting, and it put way too much emphasis on my hips and butt. Both of which I hated. "Oh, hell no," I muttered, scowling at my reflection.

Cammy peered over my shoulder. Her bubblegum pink hair clashed wildly with the color of the one-shoulder dress I had on. "I agree. The color is bad and the fit isn't flattering. That's a no." She spun and presented her back. "Zip me up, will ya?"

I tugged the zipper on her black dress that had a simple off the shoulder top and a massive explosion of a skirt. The netting was a very fine texture, and the length of the A-line skirt fell to right above her ankles.

"I think that's too short for you," I said.

"No, it's not short enough." Cammy considered her reflection in the mirror. "I'm thinking I might cut it off to right above my knees, maybe add some star appliques, and a few sequins on the netting of the skirt."

I nodded. "That's a great idea."

"It's a bargain for forty bucks." Cammy grinned. "Come on Ella, try on something else."

"Why am I not surprised that you went for the witchy, black dress?"

"It contrasts nicely with my hair."

I reached for the next gown. It was a pale dusty blue. "I like the style of this one."

"I thought it might look good with your coloring."

While Cammy changed back into her clothes,

I struggled with the blue dress. I managed to get my arms in the sleeves and then got stuck trying to ease it over my head. "I need some help, please!" My voice was muffled under layers of tulle.

"Hang on." Cammy came around and started tugging the dress down.

It slipped into place. I checked the mirror and was pleasantly surprised. The gown was romantic, with long sheer sleeves. The off-the-shoulder style was actually quite flattering. The bodice was a tad snug, but it made my waist look smaller. The tulle skirt poofed out, effectively hiding my butt, and the long skirt swept down to the floor with a bit of a flounce at the hem.

"I dig this one!" Cammy said, looking at my reflection in the mirror. "Your waist looks tiny, and it has a definite Cinderella vibe."

This could work... I considered the dress but spotted a tear in the flounce. "It's torn, though."

Cammy knelt down. "It's on the seam. I can fix this easily."

I checked the tag hanging from the sleeve. It was seventy percent off. "I like the price."

Cammy stood behind me and scooped up my long blonde hair. "You should wear your hair up, with a few curls falling in tendrils."

This dress definitely sets an old fashioned, dreamy and sort of faery tale tone... I smiled at my reflection in the mirror. "I don't even look like myself in this."

My younger sister grinned at me. "Isn't that the whole point of the masquerade party?"

I spun back to the mirror. *Max was never going to know what hit him,* I decided.

***

The night of the party had arrived. I stood in my room, wearing the dusty blue gown. I'd tamed my wavy hair into a partial updo, and as Cammy suggested, I tugged a few blonde tendrils loose to curl around my face. My cosmetics were much heavier than usual. I wore a smoky eye, and deliberately left my lip color pale.

I was nervous, no doubt about it, and even more jumpy for what I was about to attempt. Tonight was a do or die. One way or another my destiny would be decided, but even a wise woman knows that sometimes you need to give fate a bit of a nudge.

As a daughter of Midnight, I knew my share of wise woman charms and spells. I typically worked with the quieter magicks. Hearth and home type stuff, or kitchen witchery, some folks would call it. I knew how to bump up a dish with enchanted herbs to encourage healing or comfort. In a pinch, I even used magick to bolster my creativity when I was having trouble with a design project, and sure, I'd worked prosperity magick to bring in new clients when money was tight...but what I was about to attempt? This was brand new territory for me.

My intention was to work a confidence spell on myself—or what could be classified as a glamour. I'd sat up for hours perfecting the wording, considering the proper way to go about it, and my decision was made. I would cast a spell on the mask I'd be wearing to the party.

It seemed like the safest route to take, as I wouldn't be breaking the non-manipulation rule, since I wasn't casting a spell *on* Max. I was casting the spell on myself. With the intention to be beautiful, assertive and brave enough to admit how I felt, and to act on it. That way Max would see me as a desirable, confident woman instead of 'good old Ella', his friend.

His best friend. My conscience warned.

"I've waited so long. The spell is only to make *me* bolder, nothing more." I reminded myself. "Besides, how much trouble can a little magick cause?" With a deep breath, I picked up the mask and tied it on. I secured the ribbons with a few pins, and at last I went to the long oval mirror and took in the whole costume.

An exotic stranger stared back. "Well, Gabriella Midnight...just look at you." I smiled, delighted at the dramatic transformation. The off the shoulder style paired with a modest sweetheart neckline, making my neck look slender and longer. I ran my hands over the floral appliques sewn over the sheer blue mesh of the skirt and felt like a sexy princess.

"Mild mannered graphic designer by day," I said to my reflection, "sassy enchantress by night." I adjusted one sleeve by the cuff and nodded in satisfaction at how the whisper soft sleeves were flowing. I turned around, looked over my shoulder and checked the illusion corset at the back. My waist appeared smaller and my backside—the bane of my existence— seemed wonderfully shaped beneath the layers of tulle.

Inspection complete, I took a deep breath and faced the long mirror again. Resting my fingertips on the bottom of the dark blue mask, I carefully recited the spell that I'd written down.

"With these words I now weave a charm so true; glamour bound to a mask of midnight blue. May this spell catch his eye and bolster my heart; a confidence spell cast with a wise woman's art. Let him finally see me as I wish to be seen; a desirable woman, and not merely a dream. No longer his friend, but a lover both brave and bold, may a new life begin from the ashes of the old."

My fingertips grew warm and I gently lowered my hands to the dresser. With intention, I closed up the spell. "By the powers of earth, air, water and fire; elements four, grant me my desire."

I felt a tingle in my fingers as I sealed the spell. Nodding to myself in the mirror, I tucked the paper with the written spell safely away in my dresser drawer. I slipped my feet into a pair of silvery flats and headed downstairs to catch a ride to the party with Cammy and Gran.

***

The old ruins of the Marquette family home brooded at the top of Notch Cliff. The house had originally been built almost one hundred and eighty years ago. The majority of the stone structure had survived wind, rain, time...and even a fire. At some point decades ago, one section of the roof had caved in, and now construction scaffolding ran across half of the front of the mansion. Restoration was underway.

I stood back and studied the timeworn building. The modern scaffolding should have appeared industrious, but the gothic stone manor still maintained it's aura of spookiness. It had been dramatically up lit for the event, and the old manor home created an enigmatic backdrop for the party.

"Come on, slowpoke!" Camilla called to me, tossing her head. She held Gran's arm as they made their way toward the music and laughter of the guests. She looked wonderful, and a little rock and roll with her tousled pink hair and short black party dress. Gran had chosen a lavender, georgette jacket dress. It fell to her knees in asymmetrical layers, and the sleeves of the jacket were long and flattering. Gran carried a silver mask on a stick, and they'd barely arrived when Drusilla, Garrett, and Brooke greeted them.

I remained further back and watched my family. In a tea-length, lace dress of dusty rose, Drusilla simply shone. Garrett stood by her side in a navy suit with his eleven-year-old ward, Brooke. The girl was all smiles in her simple, lilac colored, fit and flare dress and was chatting happily with Cammy.

I lifted my face to the waxing moon and reminded myself to be brave. "Faint heart never won prince charming." I psyched myself up. *Come on girl, you want passion and romance?*

Stop stalling and go get your man. My silent pep talk did the trick. I lifted my chin and slowly walked across the grass toward the lights and the party.

Music was playing, and a few couples were already slow dancing on the stone terrace. I eased closer to the gathering and spotted Max. He was chatting at the edge of the patio with a dark-haired man who was wearing a top hat and steampunk style outfit. The party itself was arranged between the partially restored stone terrace and a huge white tent that had been erected on the grass to hold the party goers. I stepped onto the stone terrace, and the trim man Max had been talking to nodded to me in acknowledgment.

Part of me was flattered to have caught such a good-looking man's attention, but the rest of me only had eyes for Max. *See me!* I thought, and as if I'd willed it, Max turned and looked straight at me. My heart beat faster seeing him all dressed up. He rarely put on a suit, but he wore the dark suit and white shirt very well. He hadn't worn a tie, and that didn't surprise me at all.

While I'd been busy staring at Max, the man in the top hat walked directly to me. His black hair brushed the top of his shoulders, and a cravat was tied at his neck. He wore a double breasted burgundy vest over a white poet shirt and dark slacks. Now that he was closer, I noticed that his top hat was made from leather. Steampunk goggles were around the band of his hat, and tiny copper gears decorated a wine-red half mask.

"*Bonsoir, mademoiselle.*" The French accent was perfect, and he took my hand and lifted it, kissing the back of it in an old-world gesture.

I smiled. "Good evening." My voice was low and sounded surprisingly husky to my own ears.

The eyes behind the mask were a deep, dark brown, and even though he was attractive, my gaze went directly over his shoulder toward Max. The man's lips twitched, and his eyes traveled to Max and back to me. "*Bonne chance, ma belle.*" He gave my fingers the slightest of squeezes and gallantly stepped aside.

I was going to need all the luck I could get. I

lifted my eyes and found Max standing directly in front of me. The nerves in my stomach suddenly smoothed out. All the doubts and worries I'd held waiting for this moment faded away. I studied him from behind my mask and called on the courage and bravery that I'd cast for.

Tipping my face up to Max's, I felt my lips curve up in a smile. "Dance with me," I said, and willed myself to appear calm and poised. It was a risk. Max was old fashioned, I knew. He wouldn't ever be attracted to a woman who was too aggressive. I had to find the right balance.

Without a word he took my left hand and led me out on the dance floor. The dance was perfectly polite, and of course my Max would keep a socially acceptable space between us. Even though I strained for more contact with him, I told myself to be patient. When he smiled down at me, inwardly I rejoiced. The spell was working perfectly, and things were going exactly as I'd hoped.

Time stood still as we slow danced together under the stars. Part of my mind recognized the other guests, the flickering candles, and lush flowers that decorated the terrace, and the rest of it was simply lost to the warmth of his hazel eyes.

After the slow dance we eased off the dance floor. Max kept my hand gallantly tucked in the crook of his arm and escorted me to a long table where glasses of wine were waiting for the guests. Choosing a glass of white, I sipped at the wine and watched the man I'd loved for years finally look at me as if he found me beautiful and desirable.

It took everything I had not to shout, *Yes!* And do a fist pump. Things were working out even better than I had planned. *Courage and boldness.* I reminded myself. *Be brave. Speak the truth. A new life out of the ashes of the old.*

I set my glass aside. "I'd like to speak to you. Alone," I said, holding out my hand.

"I shouldn't," he said. "I came here with—"

"Hush." I cut him off gently. "Let's take a walk."

Silently, he studied me for a moment. He took my hand, and I drew him further away from the rest of the party goers. We traveled across the old stone steps, where ivy grew thick over the bannisters, and the only light was from the waxing moon overhead. I wanted privacy, and thought I'd find it in what was left of the gardens around the estate.

The music was in the distant background, and the tulle of my dress whispered as we walked together across the gravel pathway and further away from the party. Tall scraggly hedges separated us from the other guests, and eventually we found a secluded grotto with a stone bench.

I couldn't have found a more romantic spot. This was it. I tipped my face up to his. "I've waited a long time to tell you how I feel."

He tilted his head to one side. "You have?"

It was now or never. I stepped closer to him. "Kiss me," I whispered. "Please."

He peered down into my face. "There's something about you..." He sounded not quite like himself, but my heart gave one hard lurch as he slowly leaned forward.

"Max," I whispered, rising up on my tiptoes to meet him half way.

And then it happened, we kissed. Our first kiss was gentle and testing. He eased back and stared down into my eyes. Overcome with emotion, I gently laid my hands on either side of his face and drew his mouth back to mine.

The kiss became more urgent as we held each other in the moonlight. When he wrapped his arms around my waist and pulled me close, it thrilled me to my toes. I'd held back my emotions for too long, and now they exploded.

His kisses cruised over my jaw and with a groan I threw my head back, encouraging him to go lower. He didn't though, and instead Max stepped back. "We should stop," he groaned.

"You're so old fashioned." I sighed over the sweetness of the man I adored. "I love you, Max."

Max smiled down into my eyes. "You *love* me? Well, that's a little sudden. Why don't we start with your name first, and see how it goes from there?"

"*What?*" I croaked.

"What's your name?" His tone was gentle, and he leaned down to study my face. "Or should I just call you Cinderella?"

My stomach lurched. *He wasn't joking,* I realized. *He literally hadn't recognized me.*

Max reached for the ribbons that had kept my mask in place. "I want to see your face."

"Wait." I latched onto his hands. "You honestly don't recognize me?"

He frowned. "No, should I?"

Shocked and angry, I pulled the ribbons free myself, and let the mask fall. "It's me, Max. It's Ella."

His eyes went wide. "Ella?"

"Of course it's me!" I hissed.

"*Oh my god*!" Max jumped back in shock.

CHAPTER TWO

Of all the reactions I'd imagined. *Horrified* hadn't even made the list. "Wow," I managed as he stood there, gawking.

"What are you playing at?" he demanded, and wiped his mouth off with the back of his hand.

By the goddess, I thought as my stomach dropped. *He acted as if he were revolted to have kissed me.* I stared at him while all my dreams shattered and fell to pieces at my feet.

"You shouldn't have done that," he said, quietly.

"Do what?" I asked, starting to get angry. "Kiss you? Tell you that I love you?"

He flinched. "Trick me like that. You made me think you were..."

"Anyone else but me?" I finished for him. "I've waited for two years to tell you how I feel, and you're looking at me like I did something horrible."

"Ella, I..." Max trailed off. He pulled his shoulders back. "We're friends. Good friends."

"Yes we are." I squared off with him. "And I can't begin to describe how incredibly insulting it is for me to have told you that I love you, and you're standing there acting like I punched you in the balls."

"Ella, be reasonable," Max said, in a placating tone. "You don't love me,"

"Don't you dare tell me how I feel!"

Max stepped closer and took me by the shoulders. "Let me be clear," he began in the same tone a parent would use on an unruly child. "You're like a *sister* to me. I don't think of you in a romantic, or a sexual way."

Now it was my turn to flinch. "I see." I shrugged free of his hands.

"I'm here with a date for god's sake!" Max rubbed his hand over his eyes. "I can't believe this happened."

Had my spell somehow taken away his free

will? With growing dread, I grasped that maybe it had worked a bit too well. *I'd tried to be careful. The magick was only supposed to catch his eye...and to make* me *bolder.* "You're here with a date?" My voice shook as I did my best not to cry. "Sounds like a hell of a date, if you're out here in the gardens kissing me."

"I didn't know it was you!"

"So you came out here thinking you might score an anonymous hookup at the masquerade party?" Irritated, I poked him in the chest. "Thanks Max, that makes me feel tons better."

He batted my finger away and glared. "I would never do that." He drug a hand through his dark blonde hair. "You set this whole thing up. You disguised yourself and basically lured me out here...what in the world were you thinking?"

"Lured? Now just you wait a goddamn minute!" I said, firing up. "First off I didn't disguise myself. It's a masquerade party. Secondly, the fact that you are trying to play the *victim* so you can feel better about this is laughable. Jeez, Max, did I trample on your Puritan sensibilities?"

"Watch that." His voice was flat and low.

"I love you," I said it carefully and clearly. "I have for years. I thought if I told you how I felt —"

"That I would fall in line with your plans," Max finished for me. "So you dressed up like one of those women on the silly book covers you design, and figured that I'd respond like I'm a pretty boy hero from a romance novel?" He laughed, and the sound of it hurt my heart.

"There's no need to be cruel." I swiped angrily at a tear that had fallen despite my best efforts. His condescending words had hurt me deeply.

"Go home, Ella," he said. "You've embarrassed the both of us enough for one night, don't you think?"

"You should go back to the party, Max," I said, softly. "I'm sure your date is wondering where you are. You don't want to keep her waiting."

"I'm going to forget that this ever happened." Max tugged on the lapels of his jacket. "I suggest you do the same." He stepped back and began to walk toward the lights and noise of the party. Max stopped once, glanced over his shoulder at me, and then increased his stride.

I waited until I was sure he was gone and dropped down to the stone bench. "Oh my goddess," I whispered, feeling my heart break.

"He thinks of me like a sister?" I shook my head. "His *sister*?" I simply couldn't believe it. As I replayed the whole fiasco in my mind, I thought how he'd literally wiped my kiss from his mouth. It was humiliating, it was *infuriating*, and as I sat there, something inside me broke free.

I was a daughter of Midnight, damn it. Descended from strong and powerful wise women. If Max Dubois thought I would run home with my head down because he'd refused my—romantic advances—I suppose you'd say, he had another thing coming.

"So, he didn't want me?" I said out loud. "Fine. I've wasted enough time on him, and I'll be damned if he's going to shame me into hiding." I jumped to my feet and snatched the midnight blue mask from the grass. "I'll make him sorry he treated me this way."

With my head held high, I marched back

toward the Marquette mansion. I'd duck in a bathroom and repair my face, I decided. Then I'd go get myself a drink. "Max Dubois," I muttered, stalking forward into the protective shadows of the house, "you're going to look back on this day, and bitterly regret that you let me slip right through your fingers! You thick headed, idiotic, son of a—"

The rest of my rant was cut off on impact. "Ooof!" I grunted as I bounced off the chest of a man. Without thinking, I swung my fist where I estimated a head would be.

The man countered my wild swing with a casual strength. "*Facile.*" His top hat toppled to the ground.

His mask was gone, but I recognized the French gentleman from before. I relaxed slightly. "Sorry," I said.

"*Facile*—easy," he repeated, closing his hand over my fist. "I only wanted to see if you are alright."

"I'm sorry, sir," I said. "I thought you were someone else."

His eyes traveled over my face. "And your first instinct was to throw a punch at this 'someone else'?"

"He deserves it," I said, my voice breaking a little. Embarrassed, I bore down and cleared my throat.

The man's entire posture and expression changed. I blinked as the man in front of me transformed from a suave sophisticate, to completely terrifying. His eyes flashed. Even in the darkness I could see it. "Did he hurt you?" His voice was tight, controlled.

"My feelings, yes," I admitted. "But physically, no, he did not."

"Perhaps you *should* have done as you said, and punched him in the balls."

"You heard all that?" I winced.

"I'm afraid so."

I shut my eyes. "Terrific."

"Do not be embarrassed," he said. "You were magnificent." His fingers loosened, and his grip on me was gentle. If I didn't know better, I'd have thought his fingers caressed my hand slightly as he let go.

I considered the attractive man before me. "Thank you," I said slowly.

"I suppose that I should apologize for having

intruded on your privacy." He tipped his head, deferentially, but it was clear that he wasn't sorry.

"But you won't apologize," I predicted.

His lips curved up slightly. "No, and I'm not sorry. Not in the least. As you are a guest in my home, it is my duty to see to your personal safety."

"*Your* home?" Now, I was confused.

"Yes, this is my home. Such as it is." He smiled.

With an effort, I pulled myself together. "Well then, since this is your house, would you mind showing me to a powder room? I need to fix my face." I tried to sound matter of fact.

"There's no need. You look lovely, Gabriella."

My name sounded more exotic with the French accent, and I fought against a smile. "How do you know my name?"

"I know your name because we've been corresponding online for months. You designed my company's website. I'm Philippe," he said.

"Phill-eep? I tried to pronounce the name the way he had.

"*Oui,* Philippe Marquette."

I swung my eyes back toward the Marquette house. Everything clicked. Here at last was the mysterious third of the *Trois Amis.* "You're Philippe Marquette?"

"Yes."

"I thought you'd be older," I heard myself say.

"I'm older than I look." He laughed.

I found myself smiling at the sound of his laugh. "Nice to finally meet you in person, Mr. Marquette."

"*Enchanté,*" he picked up my hand and pressed a kiss to the back of it. "Please, call me Philippe."

"Okay, Philippe." I felt a thrill, a flutter in my gut, from the old-world gesture. It was somewhat strange being face to face with a man I'd only known through correspondence, but there was something about him.

"Allow me to escort you back to the festivities." Graciously, he offered me his arm, and I accepted it.

Well, he was absolutely charming, I decided.

He led me back to the party, and I excused

myself to go use some of the fanciest porta-potties I'd ever seen. They were like miniature trailers, and outfitted with a sink, long counter and mirror. I washed my hands and was relieved to see that my makeup was holding. I patted under my eyes with a tissue and deliberately tied the mask back on.

I studied my reflection. *Maybe the spell hadn't worked the way I'd wished for, but at least now I knew the truth. I'd intended the mask to make me bold, and to give me courage, hadn't I?* Securing the pins in my hair, I squared my shoulders.

By the moon and stars, I wouldn't turn tail and run. Taking a deep breath, I went back out to join the party. I'd go find my family and get through the evening.

I went directly for the food and drink. Chatting with Brooke and Cammy, I nibbled on canapés and drank a couple glasses of white wine. I checked for my elegant host. He was on the move, going from group to group and keeping his guests content. The two glasses of wine had given me a nice, warm sensation, and I started to feel better, looser maybe, and I picked up a third.

I was standing at the edge of the dance floor, watching Drusilla and Garrett dance, when I heard a familiar low and accented voice. "May I have this dance?"

I turned and found Philippe Marquette. Beyond him, in the distance I could see Max frowning directly at me.

I deliberately shifted my attention back to Philippe. "I'd love to," I said.

With a quick spin, he led me onto the dance floor. I laughed at the fancy move, and he grinned. He knew how to dance, and he moved well in the box step as we waltzed counter-clockwise across the terrace. People were staring at us as we danced, and I didn't give a damn.

I caught a glimpse of Max. He was standing, his arms crossed over his chest, and he was livid.

I tossed my head. *That's right Dubois,* I thought. *Here's someone who doesn't cringe at being in my arms.*

Philippe pulled me a bit closer to get my attention. In response, I met his eyes, smiled up into his face, and was determined to enjoy myself.

My skirts swirled around as we danced to Lionel Richie crooning, 'Hello'. My confidence returned as we danced in time to the old song, and I began to truly *feel* beautiful, desirable, brave, and powerful. It was a wonderful, almost magickal moment. As the song ended, Philippe dipped me back with a flourish.

He held me in the dip, and for a split second, I wondered if the spell had gotten away from me. *I'd cast that spell to be seen as a desirable woman,* I reminded myself. Judging from the Frenchman's reaction, it appeared to be working. There was a smattering of applause from the party goers. "You're good," I said to him.

Philippe eased me back upright. "*Ma belle,* you've barely tried me."

My stomach gave a funny sort of twist, even as I recognized that what I was feeling was: attraction. "Is that an offer?" I heard myself say.

Philippe's eyes seemed to burn as he studied my face. "Be careful," his voice was low and made goose bumps break out on my arms.

The music stopped and we stood in the middle of the dance floor. I studied his face from behind my mask. "And if I'm tired of being careful?" I asked, trailing my fingers over the ends of his long hair where it rested on his shoulder.

He tensed. "You have no idea, Gabriella, what I might ask of you." He took my hand, kissed my fingers, and tucked my hand in the crook of his arm. Together, we left the dance floor.

I thought over his warning as we began to walk sedately back to the tables. The tempo of the music picked up and Cammy shimmied her way past me, heading for the dance floor. My sister always was the life of the party.

"Come on, Ella!" She yanked me with her.

I recognized the song and I couldn't resist joining her out on the dance floor. "I'll be back," I called to Philippe, as I was dragged along.

"Go," he said. "Enjoy yourself."

'Perfect Illusion' was throbbing out of the speakers, and feeling a deeper connection to the song than I ever had before, I threw myself into the dancing. A few moments later, Drusilla and Brooke joined us.

I tossed back my head and laughed when Cammy let out a cheer. Brooke was grinning from ear to ear. She started to giggle when Garrett joined us. The last thing I'd ever expected was Garrett Rivers to bust a move, but he wasn't too bad.

The song finished, and I waved off Cammy's attempts to keep me out there. I worked my way through the crowd, and back toward where Philippe sat at a table. He was watching me steadily. I smiled directly at him and suddenly, I found my way blocked.

"What do you think you're doing, dancing like that?" Max's voice was angry and low.

"Aww, you don't like Lady Gaga?" I asked sarcastically. "Too provocative for you?"

"Don't be stupid, Ella." Max leaned in closer, lowering his voice. "Do you have any idea who you were dancing with earlier?"

I scoffed and waved him away. "Go back to your date, Max." I started to brush past him and he surprised me by taking my arm in a firm grip.

"I'm taking you home."

"You had your chance to *take me home* earlier," I said, yanking away. "If memory serves, you turned me down and stood there playing the horrified virgin."

I heard a few couples nearby began to chuckle at that. Part of me recognized that I was probably too loud. But I didn't give a damn. I'd worked hard over the years to be seen as mild-mannered and polite. But my sarcastic bitch side had ripped loose, and I found it incredibly satisfying.

"Keep your voice down, Ella," Max said, suddenly realizing there were many curious eyes on us. "You're making a spectacle of yourself."

That did it. "You want to see a spectacle?" I reached for a glass of wine on a nearby table. "Fuck you, Max," I said, tossing the contents right in his face.

An audible gasp was heard from the party goers, and Max stood stock still while the wine ran down his face and dripped all over his shirt. Someone, somewhere, began to clap.

"Excuse us." Philippe Marquette stepped

forward smoothly and slipped a gentle arm around my waist. "Come with me, *ma belle*."

I allowed him to take the empty glass and lead me away from the party. Like magick, the crowd parted for us. Maybe that was out of respect to their host...or maybe people were afraid I'd throw another drink. I bit my lip and fought against very inappropriate laughter as we traveled further into the shadows of the nearby house.

I couldn't believe I'd done that. Tossed a drink in Max's face. Right there in front of everybody. My shoulders began to shake as I held back giggles.

Philippe rubbed my arm consolingly. "It's alright, don't cry."

"That's not helping," I warned him and then burst out laughing. I simply couldn't hold it back any more. "Quiet, polite, and dependable Gabriella Midnight, just made a scene in public!" I fanned a hand in front of my face. "Wow. What a rush!"

"I'd say he had it coming."

"Honey, you have *no* idea." I tried to catch my breath. "First he didn't want me and, now apparently he doesn't want anybody else to have me either."

"He's a foolish man to have turned down your offer of love," Philippe said so seriously that my laughter died and I glanced over at him warily.

"Um, thanks?" I said.

I wasn't sure what to make of the man. I barely knew him, yet was attracted to him despite the fact. I considered Philippe as he stood there in those old-world clothes, and they suited him perfectly. A breeze ruffled his hair, and he tossed it out of his eyes as he studied me.

Philippe's gaze traveled from the top of my head and down to the hem of the gown. His eyes slowly returned to my face, and I was suddenly very glad I still wore the mask. The way he looked me over was making me blush. What had he said earlier? *You have no idea, Gabriella, what I might ask of you.* I barely managed to repress a delicious shudder.

"Well," I said, trying to ease the sudden tension. "That should keep everyone in the village talking for the next month."

"We could give them something else to talk about," he said, and the next thing I knew, he'd pulled me in his arms and was kissing me soundly.

It was absolutely the most devastating kiss I'd ever experienced. With a moan, I gripped his shoulders for balance and opened my mouth. His tongue swept in to claim mine. Desire like I'd never known rushed through me, making my head spin. The kiss went on and on. I had no idea how long we'd been kissing in the shadows of the old house, and I didn't care.

He lifted his mouth from mine, and I found he was studying my face intently. "Gabriella," he whispered.

"Umm hmm?" I felt befuddled. But I knew one thing for sure, I wanted another of those kisses. I rose up on my tiptoes. "Kiss me again, Philippe."

He gave me a gentler kiss this time. I stepped closer, and kept moving until my chest was right against his. His mouth shifted to my forehead and he swept butterfly kisses across my face.

Blindly I reached out to toy with the ends of

his hair. I threaded my fingers through, exploring the textures. "You smell good," I said, inhaling deeply.

He began to brush kisses over my jawline, and experimentally, I pressed a kiss to the side of his neck. I trailed my tongue along his pulse, and he shuddered. I groaned at his reaction, thrilled that I was able to make him tremble.

His hand wandered down to my waist and he pulled me in even tighter. Now snugged up against his hips, I knew without a shadow of a doubt that he wanted me. "I'm trying to be a gentleman," he said.

I almost smiled. "Who asked you to be a gentleman?"

His hands ran over my back, and he bent his head and began to nibble his way across my shoulder. He dragged his teeth across the nape of my neck and I shivered, letting my head fall back.

"I am not your Max," he said, starting to kiss his way past my collar bones.

"Thank the goddess you're not." I shuddered and tightened my fingers in his hair. *Maybe the spell was working after all,* I thought. *Hadn't I cast for a lover both brave and bold?*

His mouth hovered above the swell of my breasts "I won't stop with a few kisses, Gabriella." As if to illustrate his point, Philippe bit down ever so slightly.

"To be clear," I managed to say, "I didn't ask you to stop."

"If you offer yourself to me, you're mine." His hands swept up and over my breasts.

"I can't breathe," I whispered. "I can't even think when you do that." A small part of my brain processed his words as a warning, and the rest of me was too wrapped up in the incredible pulse of desire that had my knees turning to jello. I began to shake in reaction and tightened my grip in his hair.

"Be mine, Gabriella." That low, accented voice had me quaking. "Tonight, be mine."

"Yes," I said, recklessly.

In response, Philippe bent me back over his arm. His kiss forced my head back and he damn near swallowed me whole.

CHAPTER THREE

I'd never been kissed that way before. Like the man could've devoured me right on the spot. It was *thrilling*. He scooped me up off the ground and turned with me in his arms. His mouth never left mine and I jumped when he pushed an old door of the house in.

He yanked his mouth away for a second. "Gabriella?" His voice was guttural as he hesitated on the threshold.

"Philippe?" I studied his face. It was drawn and a muscle ticked in his jaw. "What is it?" I asked.

"See me for who I am. Be sure."

A thrill of power coursed though me. Caught firmly in his arms I felt desired, beautiful, and ultra feminine. I tightened my arms around his neck. "I'm sure," I said simply. "I want to be with you tonight."

Philippe kissed me once, hard and urgently, then he carried me across the threshold.

He set me on my feet once we were inside, and shoved the door closed behind us. The heavy old door screeched across the floor and I squinted in the darkness.

"Come with me." He took my hand, pressed a kiss to the back of it, and I followed where he led.

Silently we moved down a hallway that had to have been original to the house. As my eyes adjusted, I noticed the moonlight filtering in through the old wavy glass of the windows. We passed several empty rooms and eventually arrived at huge wooden staircase.

I paused long enough to raise the skirt of my gown to more easily navigate the stairs. We walked up the steps, gained a landing, and I saw the glitter of broken glass. A huge stained-glass panel had once decorated the landing at some point, and now a large section had plywood attached over it. I gulped as we continued to climb the staircase, and part of me felt like I was traveling back in time.

Now on the third floor, Philippe began to stride purposefully down a corridor. This area was scrupulously clean, and even in the darkness I had the impression that this section of the house had been restored, as there were the faintest scents of paint and wood stain in the air.

Philippe stopped before a tall door and slowly pulled an ornate key from the pocket of his slacks. He unlocked it and I followed him inside. When he locked the door behind us, the sound had my heart racing, not in fear, but in anticipation.

He moved easily in the dark room and I heard the scrape of a match. Philippe stood lighting candles that were arranged across a huge stone mantle. One by one he lit them, and I studied him carefully as he did. His hands were rock steady, and he appeared elegant and confident.

The candles illuminated the room better than I would have expected. I stepped deeper into the room and saw a huge leather sofa and a chunky coffee table. An old Persian rug softened the hardwood floor. I ran my fingers across the arm of a pretty wingback chair, and when I lifted my eyes he was standing in front of me, untying the cravat at his throat.

"You won't think of him," he said. "When I am finished with you, you won't even remember his name."

Yes, please. I thought, watching as he unbuttoned the vest.

Slowly he took me in his arms, but to my surprise, he turned me around. "Allow me," his voice rumbled, and his hands began to work at the fasteners at the back of my dress.

"Philippe." I groaned when his mouth brushed down the right side of my neck. Reaching back I sank my hand in his hair, holding his mouth at the nape of my neck.

I felt the dress give way and with a little push the dress began to slide down my arms. Philippe's mouth followed the dress. I started to try and tug at the cuffs of the sleeves and he was there, smoothing them over my hands. The skirt caught at my hips and for a second my confidence faltered. His hands were running over the long line strapless bra I'd worn. He slid his hands down, and eased the dress over my hips, where it pooled at my feet.

I stood before him in the bra and a pair of lace underwear that stretched over my wide hips. His hands skimmed my curves, and helplessly, I arched my back.

"*Ma belle*," he murmured. I jolted when he dropped to his knees and began to run kisses down my spine and over my backside. "*Je te veux*," he whispered.

"What did you say?" I asked as he rose to his feet behind me. His hands began to deftly unhook my bra. "I don't understand," I began, and my breath caught when he peeled the bra away, pulled my backside firmly against him, and wrapped his hands over my breasts.

"I want you," he said in my ear, as one of his hands trailed lower.

"I want you, too." I stretched my head back to kiss him and he dipped his fingers past my panties and touched me. "God!" I bucked against him.

His roving hands had my arms hanging useless at my sides. "Just let me..." he murmured in my ear and tugged the lace away.

"You are beautiful," he said, and my knees went weak.

I began to pant, trying to hold on to my sanity. Meanwhile, he continued to kiss and scrape his teeth across the nape of my neck. "Philippe," I said. "Let me touch you."

He released me and I spun in his embrace. I reached for the vest and shoved it off his arms, while he continued to torment me with hot kisses and his hands running over my butt. The poet shirt frustrated me, there were no buttons on the front. "Take off the shirt," I urged him, and nipped his bottom lip.

"So demanding," he chuckled.

I reached for the waistband of his slacks and before I knew what had happened, I found myself dipped backwards until he lay me back on the rug. He rose up, smiled, and pulled the shirt over his head.

Oh my god, was my one clear thought. He was beautiful, with lean muscles and a strip of dark chest hair. I reached for him, but with a sexy smile, he evaded me and instead shrugged off the last of his clothes. I held my arms out to him, and at last he knelt at my feet. Slowly, ever so slowly, he settled between my thighs.

I let my legs drop open to accommodate his hips, thinking he'd move to claim me immediately. But he didn't. Instead, he untied the ribbons from the mask and tugged it free. "I want to see you," he said. "No more masks, Gabriella." He kept his lower body still, and I moved my hips restlessly beneath him. I felt him brush against my entrance and I gasped.

I tugged on one of his hips, and he pressed forward the tinniest bit. "Philippe," I whispered. "Don't tease me."

He rested on his elbows and continued to search my face. "Are you in such a hurry then?" he smiled.

Getting frustrated, I grabbed ahold of his long hair and tugged his face closer. "For you? Yeah, I am in a—" My words halted when he pressed forward a bit more.

"Gabriella," he whispered my name and stroked the hair back from my face. His eyes were locked on mine when he slid deep inside.

I heard someone scream and realized it had been me. My back arched off the carpet and he began to move.

I moved helplessly against him and he gentled me with a soft kiss. "No need to rush. We have all night *ma belle*."

"I'm never going to make it." I gasped out as he set a leisurely pace.

"Yes, you will." He smiled. "Trust me."

***

I woke up and found I was under a chenille blanket, still on the carpet, and snuggled beside Philippe Marquette. He was sprawled on his back and holding me against his right side with one arm. I eased up on my elbow and studied the Frenchman. While he wasn't conventionally handsome, I had to admit, the man simply 'did it' for me. At the moment his face was relaxed and he was snoring the tiniest bit.

I grinned down at him. Philippe had said we had all night, and he'd been a man of his word. I had to give him an A+ for stamina.

Gently, I reached out and ran my fingers over the line of dark hair that ran down the center of his chest. Our first time together had been slow and easy. He'd made me feel absolutely beautiful *and* he had driven me crazy. He never increased his pace and he'd gently worked me over the edge into a sweet orgasm.

I'd fallen asleep for a short time and he'd slowly woken me. Moving down my body, Philippe had feasted on me like a man starving. I'd held his head to me and the second orgasm had me screaming down the walls.

I'd barely managed to get my eyes to focus when he looped the back of my knees over his arms, positioned himself, and pushed inside of me. He'd set a ruthless pace that time, and I'd absolutely *loved* it.

Sighing, I ran my hand over his chest. Did I dare go for a third round? I eased my hand beneath the blanket, across his hips, and helped myself.

It only took a few minutes to rouse him. He groaned my name as I continued to explore and stroke him. I kissed my way down his chest. "More," I breathed.

He caught my hair and pulled my head up. "You better stop that."

"Why?" Deliberately, I flicked my tongue across his nipple.

His voice was tight. "Because if you don't stop, I won't be able to keep from taking you all over again."

"Maybe I'm not finished with *you*, yet." I closed my teeth around his nipple and tugged. As I watched, he closed his eyes on a hiss of pleasure.

"Gabriella, I'm trying to be a considerate lover. It's..." his breath caught when I pushed the blanket aside and gave him the slightest of squeezes. "I thought—" His voice was breathy. "I thought, maybe you might need..."

I straddled him and slowly, deliberately, slid down. Watching, as Philippe shuddered in reaction while I took him in to the hilt.

"*I'm* doing the taking this time, you gorgeous Frenchman," I said, linking my hands with his.

"You have my permission," he groaned.

I chuckled. "Third time's the charm, Philippe." Slowly and deliberately I rode him, until he came again.

An old clock chiming somewhere in the house woke me. It was still full dark and I counted four chimes.

I sat up slowly and discovered that Philippe

was gone, but the door was open. *He was probably in the bathroom,* I figured, and patted around for my things. I found my underwear and had managed to hook my bra into place when Philippe entered the room. He was carrying a bottle of wine and two glasses.

He was also nude.

My lips twitched. "Do you always waltz around the house buck naked?"

"Only when I have a beautiful maiden locked in the haunted tower to ravage." He wiggled his eyebrows at me and sounded so lascivious that I bit back a snort of laughter.

"The tower? Is that where we are?" I stepped into my dress. "And by the way...' I smiled at him. "I thought the maiden held her own in the ravaging department."

He smiled at my comment and set the wine down. "What are you doing?"

"Getting dressed." I said and eased the sleeves up. I presented my back to him. "Button me up will you?"

He stood behind me and rested his hands on my hips. "And if I didn't want you to leave yet?"

I leaned back against him with a sigh. "Philippe this was a wonderful night. You made me feel beautiful—"

"You *are* beautiful," he argued and pulled me back against him. "Do you feel what you do to me?"

My mouth dried up. *Good god, he was ready to go again.* I settled back against him with a sigh. "We can't stay up here forever."

"I want to see you again," Philippe nuzzled my ear.

My heart gave a happy bounce. "I'd like that," I whispered, and turned to kiss him.

"I only want to see you," he said solemnly. "You see no one but me, Gabriella."

"Of course." I studied his face. "I know you don't know me very well, but Philippe, I'm too honest to play games with you."

"I didn't think you were playing," he said, lowering his forehead to mine. "We came together unexpectedly, but now that I've found you..."

"I realize you may not believe me," I said. "But what happened here tonight? I've never done anything like this before. Especially not with someone I just met."

His eyes were steady on mine. "I do believe you."

"Well, that's a start."

We kissed again, and it was a while before I managed to get dressed. Eventually, we both did, and he drove me home.

Shadow the cat was waiting for me when I came in the back door. The sun still hadn't broken the horizon, and the house was quiet.

"Meow," he cried.

I patted him on his kitty head and tiptoed my way up the back stairs with the cat at my side. I shut the bedroom door silently behind me, managed to peel off the gown, and folded it over the cedar chest at the foot of my bed. I took my hair down, climbed naked into bed, curled on my side, and pulled the quilts up over my head. Exhausted and happy, I closed my eyes. Shadow jumped up, claimed a spot on my hip, and began to purr.

***

"Ella," Cammy shook my shoulder a couple

of hours later. "Ella, wake up."

I pulled the covers down from over my head. "What do you want?" I groaned.

"What did you and Max fight about last night? I'm dying to know!"

"That's private," I said and pulled the covers right back over my head.

Cammy laughed and bounced on the bed. "Did you hook up with the smoking hot French dude?"

"Camilla Jane Midnight," I said from under the covers. "Unless you want to die...Go away!"

"Oooh, you used my whole name. This must be serious!"

I groaned again.

"That sexy French guy? Phil, is that his name?" she asked.

"Philippe." I said, pulling the covers down to my chin. "His name is pronounced *Phill-eep*."

"Ooh la la." Cammy giggled. "I gotta tell you: the way you two danced together? That was the coolest thing I *ever* saw."

I started to sit up, remembered at the last second that I was naked, and tucked the sheet over my breasts. "When did you meet Philippe?"

"Garrett introduced him to the family right about the time you first danced with Max."

I cringed, thinking of the exchange in the garden with Max.

"Then you and Max took off and Philippe," Cammy continued, "he sort of ghosted."

Had Philippe been watching me the entire time? I wondered.

"Ella?" Cammy's voice broke in on my thoughts.

"Yeah?" I shoved at my wayward hair.

"Max seemed pretty angry after you left the party with Philippe."

"Oh?" I went for a casual tone.

"You know, last night was crazy. You take off with Philippe, and Max introduced us to his girlfriend. I didn't even know he was dating, did you?"

"No, I didn't," I said honestly.

Cammy patted my knee. "I always figured you'd end up with Max. Goes to show you, sometimes nothing is the way it seems."

As she bounced out of my room, I leaned

back against my pillows and had to agree.

***

Philippe had warned me the morning he'd driven me home that, with the winery opening and the grape harvest coming in August, his schedule would be fairly unpredictable.

I assured him that would be fine, I had plenty of work to do...and besides I needed to take some time and let all the changes in my life sink in. It was hard losing my best friend, and I was still wrapping my mind around the fact that I'd taken Philippe as a lover.

I did my best to go about my normal routine. To my relief, the family didn't push me on my fight with Max, or on the circumstances involving my leaving the party. I dreaded the coming Wednesday when Max typically came by for breakfast with the family. I wasn't surprised when he called the house Tuesday night saying he had an appointment and would be unable to make it.

Gran gave me a long look when she hung up the phone. "Is there any way for you to repair your friendship, with Max?" she'd asked.

"Nope." I crossed my arms. "Maybe he's having breakfast with his new girlfriend." I'd tried to sound indifferent, but deep inside, I was sad. Max hadn't missed a Wednesday breakfast with the family in six months. But I supposed those days were well past us.

Philippe and I managed to go out to lunch. He had to get back to the winery, and we'd parted with a smoldering kiss and the hope of making time for an evening alone as soon as possible.

I kept busy, taking care of the house and paying the household bills. When I checked my business account, I realized with a sick sort of dread that Max still owed me for the work I'd done on his website for Mother's Day.

His bill was a week past due and I knew it was his busy season—however, I had the trash and water bills still left to pay. I sent him a reminder email, and after another week passed, the reminder email hadn't been answered.

Determined to gather my fee, I made up my mind to drop by the garden center early Saturday morning. One of us had to be a professional.

I tossed on a pale blue shirt, my khaki shorts, and put my wavy hair in a high ponytail. I drove my Honda to the garden center knowing Max would be prepping for a busy sales day. His perennial sales during May and June often carried his business throughout the year.

I pulled in the gravel lot and saw that his lights were on in the little house he used as a storefront/apartment. I went around to the backdoor as was my habit, invoice in hand. I heard his voice and my heart sped up. My sneakers were quiet on the gravel as I walked toward the porch.

"No, honestly Garrett, I *would* recommend her for the position," Max said. "She's damn good at what she does."

Hearing the topic of his conversation, I stepped up and knocked on the back door.

Max shifted and saw me. "Yeah, I appreciate it," he said in the phone. "I'll get back to you. Thanks Garrett." He disconnected.

"Good morning." I remained on the back porch.

"Ella." With a frown, Max pocketed his

phone.

"I'm not armed." I tried a smile through the screen door. "No drinks in my hand. I promise."

Max grunted at that. "Come in, Ella."

Your invoice," I said, deliberately setting the envelope on the counter. "I know this is your busy season, but it's two weeks past due."

"Sorry about that. I've been preoccupied." He looked around as if searching for something, grabbed his checkbook from the clutter on the counter, and began to write a check.

"Why have you been preoccupied?" I asked as he wrote.

Max tore the check off and handed it to me. "There's been a few reasons."

I took the check by my fingertips, careful to avoid any accidental contact. "Has the mystery girlfriend been keeping you busy?"

"As a matter of fact, yes." He grabbed his keys from the counter and faced me. "Look what happened at the party, our argument..."

"It was ugly," I admitted.

"Agreed," he said.

"I miss you," I said, careful to keep any inflection from my voice. "I miss my best friend."

Max didn't respond, and the silence stretched out long and awkward between us.

Finally, he spoke. "If this is going to be too difficult for you, Ella, I can hire someone else to do the seasonal updates on the garden center website."

Difficult? I wondered what exactly he meant by that and took a careful breath before speaking. "Whatever makes you the most comfortable, Max."

He nodded. "I'll ask around about finding a new web designer."

I'd guessed that this might happen after *everything*, and yet, it was still more hurtful than I'd expected. "I'll let you get to work," I said, taking a step back. "Goodbye, Max." I nodded to him politely, kept my head up, and walked out the door.

CHAPTER FOUR

The next few days passed slowly. Out of the blue, Philippe called me from the airport. His younger brother had been seriously hurt in an accident, and he was flying to France to be with him.

"Take care of your family," I told him. "It's fine. Don't worry about me."

"I'll miss you, *ma belle*," he said, the frustration and the concern plain in his voice. "The cell phone service may be poor..."

"It's alright," I said. "Go. *Bon voyage*." I whipped out one of the few French phrases I knew.

It was Garrett who told me a few days later that Philippe's younger brother was an amateur race car driver. He'd been involved in a crash during a race, and it had been a bad one. Out of curiosity I did an online search and was surprised to discover that his brother, Chauncey, was a popular racer in Europe.

So, I found myself in a long-distance, on-line relationship, and it totally sucked. We exchanged emails daily and did manage a few phone calls. Philippe was worrying about being back in time for the upcoming harvest, and getting his brother set up with physical therapy, plus everything else he would need to fully recuperate. He filled me in on his brother's progress and I told him that I was staying busy with my web design... but that was a lie on my end. I was horribly lonely without Max in my life. It was humbling to realize how much his friendship had meant to me.

As for Philippe, well I wasn't even sure if what we had qualified as anything.

Maybe this long-distance thing wasn't even a relationship. We'd only had that one night together and a lunch date, before everything and everyone started conspiring against us...and I was probably being melodramatic.

The fourth of July came and went, and we

rolled into the dog days of summer. Garrett called asking me to attend a meeting so I could meet the new Public Relations person he'd hired for the winery. Delighted at the opportunity to take my mind off missing both Max and Philippe, I put on a nice floral sundress and a happy face and drove to Garrett's house.

I was sitting with Garrett and sipping a glass of iced tea in his bright kitchen. Brooke was showing off Tabby the kitten, who was growing by leaps and bounds, and I was relaxing for the first time in weeks. My laptop was open and ready to go on the big rustic farm table, and when the new PR person strolled in, I smiled automatically.

The striking brunette made me uncomfortable instantly, although I couldn't figure out why. When Garrett introduced her as Nicole Craig, I almost bobbled my glass of tea. That was a name I recognized immediately. The woman was Max's ex fiancée

This must be who Max was recommending over the phone to Garrett on the day I dropped off his invoice.

While I had never met the woman who'd broken Max's heart in person, I detested her on principal. She was tall, thin, and her dark hair was expertly highlighted. The woman had clipped in on gorgeous, high heeled sandals, and was sitting at the big farmhouse table, dressed like a million bucks.

And to make matters more infuriating, Nicole Craig seemed easy to get along with. She chatted easily with Brooke, and was warm, clever, and friendly.

It's all an act. I thought nastily. *The bitch couldn't fool me...She probably did the blonde highlights to cover up her gray hair.* Appalled at the viciousness of my inner monologue, I limited myself to the briefest of responses during the meeting.

Garrett and Nicole gave me a list of wine varieties to add to the website, and a few requests for fine tuning certain areas. Garrett requested another meeting in mid-August to make sure everything was implemented and running smoothly online.

Marching orders in place, I gave Brooke and her kitten a hug goodbye, nodded politely to

Garrett and Nicole, and went home to throw myself into my work. I needed to stay busy.

I was thrilled when an author contacted me with a request for coordinating book covers for an entire series of novels. The commission would certainly help make up for the loss of monthly income since Max had fired me. As a result, I stayed locked upstairs in my attic office and busted ass updating the winery website and designing book covers for weeks.

As time rolled toward August, I couldn't recall the heat bothering me to this extent before. I was absolutely miserable. I felt exhausted and out of sorts all the time, plus my stomach had been driving me crazy. It didn't matter what I ate, I couldn't stop burping and *everything* made me feel sick to my stomach.

Philippe had called me late one evening to tell me he would be returning to the states soon, and while I was happy to hear from him, I warned myself not to build a romance out of one night and one date.

No matter how good-looking he was, or how incredible that night had been.

I moped over my negative thoughts and

picked a huge argument with my sisters over whose turn it was to cook dinner. I ended up screaming at them, and promptly bursting into tears. Dismayed at my own behavior, I retreated to the attic and checked the wall calendar in my office, figuring I was due for an epic bout of PMS. Then I did such a hard double-take that I lost my balance.

My period was late.

My heart slammed against my ribs. I flipped the page of the calendar back one month and tried to remain calm.

"Holy shit," I breathed, staring at the calendar. I wasn't merely a few days late. I hadn't had my period in June either.

"It's got to be stress." I nodded and tried to convince myself of it. Surely all of the emotional upheaval of losing my best friend had been enough to throw me off...plus my cycle wasn't always regular.

However, it was now near the end of July, and I'd skipped not one, but *two* periods. My heart dropped to my feet. The fight with Max hadn't been the only big thing that had happened to me... A gorgeous, sexy Frenchman had "happened" as well.

"No," I said. "It's stress, that's all it is." But on the slim chance I was wrong, I decided I should be smart and double check.

I got up before dawn and drove over the Clark Bridge and into St. Charles county. I certainly couldn't go to the local grocery store. I might as well take out a billboard and advertise. I decided to hit a national chain 24-hour drug store instead, bought a pregnancy test and paid cash.

Afterwards, I drove to the nearest fast food place to use their restroom. I locked the stall door, read the directions, and peed on the stick. Replacing the cap, I stuffed the test and the box back in my purse and washed my hands. I got myself a lemon lime soda and counted my burps as I waited in the parking lot for the results.

When the timer on my phone sounded, I took a deep breath, and checked.

The test read: Pregnant.

Once I stopped crying, I lifted my head up from where I'd let it fall to the steering wheel and made an appointment with my gynecologist. My pregnancy test was confirmed the next day. I probably only heard half of what the nurse told me. Afterwards, I stood in shocked silence, while a friendly receptionist made an appointment for an ultrasound for me in two weeks.

I was sent home with a bunch of pamphlets, suggestions for vitamins, and a list of things to avoid. I locked the door of my room, dumped everything on my bed and stared at it. This didn't seem real...although I knew it was.

"I'm having trouble even making a decision about prenatal vitamins," I whispered to Shadow who sat on my bed studying me silently. "How am I supposed to know what else to do?" I gathered the cat up in my arms and muffled my sobs against his fur.

I hit the internet to research the first trimester of pregnancy and saw enough about the statistics of miscarriage that it scared the bejesus out of me. After that, I stayed off the medical websites and re-read the pamphlets from the doctor a little more carefully.

I knew that most women didn't announce their pregnancy until the end of the first trimester—and I told myself that was the wisest course of action. I needed to tell Philippe, but how would I even find him? Perhaps it would be best to sit tight and wait to see what they found out when I had my ultrasound appointment in two weeks. There was no point in getting everyone riled up... what if something happened?

But I knew. My boobs were killing me, the brutal summer heat was kicking my ass, and I struggled with horrible morning sickness. Although why they called it morning sickness I had no idea. For me it was 'all damn day sickness'.

I'd read that it was supposed to be a good sign, increasing hormones and all that, but it was god-awful. Dry toast, crackers, and pretzels helped somewhat. I didn't dare drink any herbal tea. I knew women who were expecting should be especially careful with that. Instead I sipped at ginger ale. I carried green aventurine tumbled stones in my pockets—it was supposed to be good for combatting nausea. I tried aromatherapy, but my sense of smell was so acute that it didn't seem to help.

There were plenty of mornings I knelt over the toilet dry heaving and silently prayed to whatever god was listening that I would finally throw up and get the sickness over with for the day. But that never happened.

My moods were all over the place. I cried over the silliest things and was cranky and bitchy the rest of the time. My sisters avoided me, the cat hid, and Gran told me to meditate more and not to take my bad attitude out on the family.

The month of August brought thunderstorms and more intense heat. I felt like death, and wondered bitterly where was that pregnant glow I'd always heard about? I hid the huge circles under my eyes with concealer and tried to avoid the family in the mornings when my nausea was worse. I bought an extra box fan for my office, cranked it on high, and it helped keep me a tad more comfortable. Sort of.

I almost broke down and confided in Dru the night before the ultrasound, but I didn't want to cause her any pain. Probably not the most considerate thing in the world to confide in your older sister, who couldn't have kids of her own, that you were knocked up from a single night of passion.

Besides, Drusilla was on cloud nine. She was happy in her romance with Garrett and enjoying writing her latest book. When she wasn't working, or maintaining the gardens at home, she was helping Garrett and Brooke with their new gardens.

Camilla had snagged a job at the *Trois Amis* wine shop and she was there practically full time. The rest of the time she and Gran were creating salves, lotions and soaps, and the kitchen smelled horrible to me most days. It was so vile that I held my breath when I passed through. I used to enjoy the herbal scents that they conjured up. Now it made me feel like I was going to gag.

The afternoon of my obstetrician's appointment, I tried to hide the worst of my pallor with makeup. I tugged a loose summer dress over my head, and its empire waist hid any bump that I might have. I probably didn't have one, but was paranoid about it nonetheless.

Slipping on a pair of sunglasses, I managed a

sick smile to Gran as I left, my heart pounding hard from anxiety. I walked to my car with an exaggerated casualness. "It's like being on some hardcore, undercover black-ops mission," I muttered, backing out of the driveway.

It had been hell trying to keep the secret for the past two weeks. I'd been sure that my grandmother or my sisters would catch on to what was happening. But they didn't seem to notice anything unusual—besides my bitchiness.

Maybe I was just that damn ordinary and unremarkable. First Max had rejected my affections, and I'd lost his friendship. Next, Philippe, that dark and mysterious Frenchman who'd been the most exciting lover I'd ever known, had all but disappeared.

I was on my own, and so I went to my doctor's appointment alone. Sweat ran down my back while I sat in the waiting room with my sunglasses on. I was the last patient of the day, and I prayed that I wouldn't see anyone I knew. Finally they called me back, and while the chipper ultrasound tech chatted away, I did my best not to throw up—as if I could.

"Here we go," the tech said.

I swung my head toward the monitor and stared mutely at the screen.

The tech took measurements, gave me a projected due date, and estimated how far along I was...but I already knew. Nine weeks. It had been nine weeks ago at the masquerade party when Philippe and I had made love, several times.

I laid there staring at the screen, listening to the heartbeat, and the reality of the situation sank in. That little funny shape with the big head on the monitor was my baby.

My baby.

"Oh my god," I said pressing my fingers to my mouth as I began to cry. "I'm having a baby. Everything has changed."

"Everything looks great. Congratulations." The tech smiled, and patted my shoulder.

On the way home from the doctor's office I had all my paperwork, and a few very important pictures in my purse, entitled 'Baby Midnight'. I cranked up the air conditioner in the car and tried to rehearse how I would tell my family the news.

"Guess what?" I would say and toss the ultrasound photos into the center of the dinner table during a meal. "Funny thing happened on the night of the masquerade party."

Or I could do the whole, "Sorry I've been a rampaging bitch lately...but I'm knocked up."

I laughed at myself, and my stomach roiled making me burp. "There isn't anything remotely funny about the situation," I said, simply to hear my own voice. "Crap, before I can even *think* about breaking the news to my grandmother and sisters...I have to track down Philippe and tell him first."

I pressed a hand to my belly. "Well, baby, it doesn't matter if he regrets being with me on the night of the masquerade or not. He still needs to know about you." I adjusted the car vents, allowing the a/c to hit me more fully in the face.

I was under no illusions that it would be a pleasant conversation, but I *had* to be honest with Philippe, and deal with the fall out. I didn't expect him to support me financially, or in a worst-case scenario...he might not even acknowledge the baby. But I wouldn't keep this information from him. Sitting in horrible rush hour traffic, I fretted over it all. When my phone vibrated I read the message and began to swear.

As if I didn't have enough on my mind, I'd received a text message from Nicole asking me to come to the garden center ASAP. Max didn't like the new web designer he'd hired, and they wanted me to work on the website again.

I wasn't sure if she was playing at Public Relations now for Max. But she asked me to drop by so she could discuss the changes to Max's website for the coming autumn season. Any other day I probably would have ignored her. But I was going to really need the money in the next six and a half months.

I also needed to buy some time to settle myself, *and* to decide how I was going to eventually break the news to my family. I knew it was stalling, but I wasn't ready to go home. It would probably be for the best to get this first meeting over with, though. I should be able to handle that. Since traffic was at a dead stop, I texted her back and told her I would be there within the hour.

By the time I pulled into the garden center, a nasty thunderstorm was brewing. The clouds overhead were dark gray and the sky had a sickly green tinge. We were in for a hell of a storm, and I tried not to take the timing of it all personally. The place was practically empty, but Max's truck was on site. I had barely made it on to the front porch when the first of the rain started to fall.

The doors were braced open. Swinging my purse strap over my shoulder, I stepped inside and heard Max's voice and a woman's coming from his office. I halted mid step and waited. I recognized the voice. It was Nicole. I eased to the side, out of sight, and listened.

"Sweetie, you know I'm crazy about you." Nicole's voice was husky and low. "But I don't think we should live together."

Crazy about you? I narrowed my eyes. *I knew it!* I'd suspected that they were getting back together...and I tried to remind myself that it wasn't any of my business what Max did. Especially now.

"It's been over two months," Max said. "I don't want to see anyone else."

"Well neither do I," she said. "But I'm not moving in to this tiny house, and that's final."

Max sighed. I could hear the sadness behind it all the way out in the storefront. "I don't want to lose you Nicole. Not again."

"You won't lose me," Nicole said. "I have a great position at the winery. Philippe told me last night that my trial period was over. I'm a permanent employee now. I think you should either move in to my condo with me in Grafton, *or* you need to build us a bigger house." She giggled.

"Nicole—" Max's half-hearted protestation was cut off.

I was morbidly curious as to what was happening inside that office, and I eased to the open door and discovered that Nicole was sitting on the edge of Max's desk, and she was kissing him.

Time seemed to freeze. Max was leaning forward, his forearms resting on the desk, and Nicole sat facing him. She shifted her lips from his mouth and pressed them gently to his forehead. I watched as she moved in further still, resting her temple against the crown of his blonde hair.

Max sighed again and leaned in closer to her, seeking comfort, and in response Nicole rubbed a hand over his back.

They truly loved each other. At the realization, I sucked in a breath, hard. Unfortunately, they both heard me.

Nicole straightened and smiled. "Hello Gabriella," she said.

Max focused on me and frowned. "Ella? What's wrong?"

"Nothing," I said automatically. "Nicole asked me to come by and talk to you about the website changes for the Fall/Halloween season. She said your other web designer hadn't worked out." I attempted a polite smile.

"Are you alright?" Max asked. "You look awful."

"Max!" Nicole chastised him. "That's the last thing a woman ever wants to hear." She hopped off the desk and walked forward with a smile. "Ignore him Gabriella, he's sulking because I refuse to move in here."

"I—" I tried to speak but didn't trust myself not to burst into tears. *Damn raging pregnancy hormones.* I tightened my grip on my purse strap.

"Gabriella, are you feeling okay?" I heard her voice as if from far away.

I could feel my fingernails digging into the palm of my hand. It snapped me back. "I'm not feeling well today," I said. "I'm sorry. Can we do this another time, guys?"

"Of course," Nicole said. "Would you like me to call someone for you?"

"No!" I said too sharply. "No," I said again, calmer this time.

"We can reschedule, or I can simply email you the notes." Nicole said.

Yeah," I said, wiping the perspiration from my upper lip. "Email me your notes. I'll get right on that.'

"Why don't you let me drive you home, Gabriella?" she said. "You're very pale."

"I'm fine," I brushed her kind offer aside. "I'm sorry to have disturbed the two of you."

"You didn't—" Nicole began.

I cut her off. "I heard you say that you'd spoken to Philippe Marquette," I tried to speak steadily. "Is he back in town?"

"Yes," Nicole said. "He's back and up at the house checking on the progress of the restoration."

"Maybe you should sit down, Ella," Max said. "You're as white as a ghost."

I turned my head away from the couple and left without another word.

Philippe was back and I needed to go see him. Right now.

CHAPTER FIVE

I drove straight up the road to Notch Cliff.
The winery show room was closed by the time I
pulled my car up to the gravel area beside the
Marquette Mansion and no one else was
around. The storm had refused to truly break. It
was blowing for all it was worth, rain was
spitting, clouds were rolling dramatically, and
thunder was rumbling.

I went to the main doors of the house and
knocked. I waited, and when no one answered I
pounded on the doors, and waited again.

No one was home.

"Damn it! Why would this be easy when
nothing else was?" Exhausted, my stomach
heaving, I spun back around, resting my back
against the thick doors.

In the gathering darkness, it looked like the end of the world was breaking over the cliffs, and I felt pushed to go and meet it. I needed a few moments somewhere private where no one would see or hear me. I was about to break—and I knew that when I did—it would be ugly.

I slung the long purse strap over my head so it was cross body, and ran for the cliffs. I pounded across the rough ground and long grass in my flats. I pushed myself hard, determined to be rid of all the anger and fear. I had to let all of it go.

I started to slow down as I drew closer to the edge. I was upset, but not stupid. I went as far as I dared, dropped to my knees in the grass, and cried. The storm cut loose and the rain pounded down. I didn't care, I stayed where I was, crying my eyes out. The dam had broken and I couldn't stop.

"*Ma chérie.*" I heard the deep, sympathetic voice an instant before a pair of masculine arms wrapped around me from behind. "Don't cry."

Even in the darkness of the storm I recognized Philippe and turned to him blindly. "You're back!" I wrapped my arms around his neck, held on, and cried all over him.

"What has happened?" he murmured in my ear.

He scooped me right off the ground. *Damn, he was strong.* I blinked, and discovered that he was shoving in a door of the old Marquette mansion.

I'd look back someday and wonder how in the hell he'd carried me all the way across the grass into the cool house, and had done it all so quickly. But for now I wiped the water from my face, hiccupped from crying and glanced around.

He was carrying me up that same set of old wooden stairs, like I weighed no more than a sack of groceries. He wasn't even winded. While part of me knew that wasn't right, another part of me struggled to put all of the pieces together from the last few moments.

Philippe gently set me on the sofa and crouched down in front of me. I squinted in the darkness of the room and tried to focus on him. "Gabriella," he said urgently.

"I'm sorry, what?" It sounded like a hive of bees buzzing in my head.

"Look at me." His voice was compelling.

"I'm going to be sick," I managed. I tried to focus on his face, but the room began to tilt to one side, and then I knew nothing else.

I was warm and comfortable, and I automatically snuggled more deeply under a soft blanket. I heard my own contented sigh, and with an effort I opened my eyes. Candles were flickering across a massive stone mantle, and a fire was burning in the fireplace. The flames created dancing shadows and light across the walls of the paneled room

I knew this room—I'd spent hours in June having all sorts of mind blowing sex with a gorgeous Frenchman here. I rubbed my eyes and came to the awkward realization that I was damn near naked under that soft blanket. Startled, I sat straight up.

Philippe was instantly there and easing me back down against the pillows. "Gabriella."

"Philippe." I tried to remember what had happened. "Aw crap, did I pass out?" I asked.

"Yes," Philippe said simply. He twisted the top off a bottle of water and handed it to me. "Drink something. You're very pale."

I took the water. "Thank you," I said and took a sip.

"I've missed you, *ma belle*," he said with a smile, and ran a finger down my cheek.

Oh boy, I thought. "Philippe." I tried to sound firm. "Where is my dress?"

"It was soaked. I took it off you and hung the dress up to dry."

"You took my dress while I was unconscious?"

"*Ma belle,*" he chuckled. "I've seen your body before."

Which is precisely how we'd gotten into this mess, I thought.

"Gabriella, what are you fretting over?" He rubbed his thumb between my brows. "You have a line here."

"We need to talk."

"You have my attention," he said. "Believe me." He stayed where he was, easily crouching between the big leather sofa and a heavy coffee table.

"Can I borrow a shirt?" I was trying not to be prudish about my lack of clothing, but I would have felt better being in something other than only my bra and underwear, considering the conversation we were about to have. *God, my purse!* I suddenly remembered what was inside of it. "I have to go get my purse," I said.

"Your purse is here." He tipped his head toward where it rested on a nearby coffee table. "Your phone has been ringing almost continuously."

On cue my cell phone began to ring again. Without a word he handed me the purse and I unzipped it and reached for my cell phone. I pulled the phone out and the paperwork from the doctor's office came out with it, landing in my lap.

I snapped my eyes up to his and his expression remained neutral. "Answer your phone, Gabriella," he suggested calmly.

My fingers felt clumsy and my heart began to pound in embarrassment. By the time I was able to get them to work, I'd missed the phone call. I checked my messages and saw several texts from my sisters, all of them wondering where I was.

I quickly typed a group text to Dru and Cammy: *I'm fine. Having a meeting with a client.* I switched the phone to silent.

I raised my eyes to his, trying to decipher the expression on his face. He remained where he was, unnaturally still.

Finally he spoke. "Are you well?"

I frowned over the phrasing. "Everything is fine according to the doctor."

"When did you see a doctor?"

"Today." I swallowed nervously. "I need to tell you something, and I don't know how else to do this. Other than to be honest and tell you flat out."

His dark eyes flickered. "What is it?"

"You should see these," I said, and pulled the ultrasound photos out from inside of the folded papers. My hands shook as I passed them over.

Calmly, he lifted the two photos. He studied them silently for a few moments while my heart pounded and my stomach churned.

"Those are from today," I explained. "The doctor says I'm nine weeks along."

"Nine weeks?" His eyes shifted to mine. "The night of the masquerade party."

"Yes." I nodded, feeling my face flush in embarrassment. "I'm pregnant Philippe. You're going to be a father."

"A father..." his voice trailed off as he continued to study the ultrasound photos.

"I hope you'll believe me when I tell you I haven't been with anyone else. The baby is absolutely yours."

"I believe you," his voice was soft, and utterly convincing.

I blinked. "You do?"

His eyes met and held mine. "Yes."

"I was afraid you wouldn't," I admitted, totally thrown off guard by his reaction. "Just so we're clear, I don't expect anything from you. I don't want any money, but still, I thought you should know," I babbled on. "I'm prepared to raise the baby on my own."

"Over my dead body," Philippe said mildly.

Alarmed, I sat up quickly. The sudden movement had the room spinning. "Damn it!" I held on to the side of the couch and waited for the room to stop revolving.

I didn't see him stand up, but before I knew it he had reached behind me and propped another pillow behind my back. Smoothly, he eased my knees over to the side and sat on the edge of the couch next to me. "Breathe slowly," he suggested. "In through the nose for a four count. Hold it for another four, then slowly blow out the air through your mouth."

While I did as he suggested he patted my knee, which was more comforting than sexual. "How severe is your morning sickness?" he asked conversationally.

I let my head fall back on the pillow. "Somewhere between 'the wrath of god', and 'someone please shoot me now'."

"What did the doctor say about that?" he wanted to know.

"They told me to let it run its course." I burped. "Sorry," I said.

He waved the burp away. "Don't be silly."

I pressed a hand to my gurgling stomach. "Since I'm *not* throwing up they don't want to give me anything unless it gets worse."

"Those bastards," he said mildly, and I couldn't help it, I began to smile.

"You're taking this awfully well," I said.

"What did you expect, Gabriella, that I'd demand a paternity test and accuse you of wanting my fortune—such as it is?"

"Well, I don't know. You keep on surprising me...and I really need to try..." I burped again. "Not to heave all over your living room carpet."

He stood and walked across the room. To my surprise he pushed a panel on a console, and a mini fridge door opened up. He pulled out a can of ginger ale, popped the top and brought it over to me.

"I'll do *anything* you want if you let me have that soda." I said reaching for it.

"Be careful," he stopped and considered me. "I might take you up on that."

I took the can and sipped. My stomach continued to gurgle loudly, and I tried not to be embarrassed.

"Besides the doctor and the two of us, who else knows?" Philippe asked, crouching beside me once more.

"No one." I sipped again. "I only had the pregnancy confirmed two weeks ago."

"I should have been here," Philippe murmured and smoothed my hair back.

I frowned at the tender gesture. "When they made an ultrasound appointment, I decided to wait and make sure everything was okay before

I told anyone."

"You shouldn't have been alone." His dark eyes studied my face. "The next appointment you have, I *will* be there."

"You don't have to—"

He cut me off. "I will be there. That's non-negotiable."

I was going to argue, but the sound of the thunder crashing and rain battering against the house became suddenly louder. I focused on the fire and the candles. "Is the power out or something?"

"It is." Philippe smiled. "I have you all alone again, *ma belle*."

"I'm not afraid of you, Philippe." I sighed. "It's not like I can get into any more trouble than I already am."

He chuckled, took my hand, and kissed it. "If you weren't so pale and feeling poorly, we'd have a proper reunion."

My jaw dropped. "Well, I..." *He wanted to make love?* My mouth worked a few times and I tried to think of something to say.

He leaned in. "I find, Gabriella, that I want you more than ever before."

My breath rushed out. "So, what, you're into pregnant women?"

"I am into *you*," he corrected, and dropped a kiss on my forehead. "I missed you."

I felt tears well up and I blinked them from my eyes. "You don't have to say things like that." I patted his arm. "It's sweet, but not necessary, Philippe."

"Gabriella, I hope *you* will believe *me*," he purposefully repeated my own words. "I am surprised at the news, but I am also happy."

A tear escaped despite my best intentions. "I...I never expected..."

"Yes, I know." He wiped the tear away himself. "Now, *mon coeur,* when was the last time you ate anything?"

"I had some toast this morning."

"That's all?"

"I was too nervous about the doctor's appointment to eat," I confessed.

"No wonder you fainted." He patted my knee and stood. "You stay right there. I'm going to make you something."

Philippe impressed me. He brought me a t-shirt of his and I slipped it over my head. It was probably weird, but having on some clothes made me feel more in control. With little fuss, he gave me some plain crackers to nibble on while he heated up some chicken soup in an old pot over the fire. Before long I had a nice mug of soup. I sipped carefully, and for the first time in a long time, my stomach settled.

"You're much kinder to me than I probably deserve," I said.

"Nonsense," he said.

"You're a good man, Philippe. You only got back into town and now you're dealing with your one-time hookup showing up pregnant and crying on your doorstep."

"You were never my 'one-time hookup'. He leveled me with a stern look. "Please don't ever say that again."

I watched him tending to the fire as I sipped my soup. He stood with his back to me framed by a massive stone fireplace. Above the mantle, I noticed for the first time a large painting. A striking man stared back from the portrait. He was portrayed standing with the Marquette Mansion in the background, as it had been a long time ago. I'd estimated the subject of the painting to be in his twenties. His dark hair was long, his clothes were elegant and obviously he'd been a wealthy young man. While it was a striking painting, the vibes coming from it were all wrong.

"That portrait is new," I said. "I don't remember seeing it the last time I was here."

"Do you like it?"

I studied it from where I sat. "It has weird vibes, and the guy looks like a bit of a player if you ask me. Why did you buy it?"

He smiled "Actually it is not a new purchase. It is in fact quite old. This is a portrait of Pierre Michel Marquette from the 1840's."

Wow, I thought. *That's a hell of an antique to have casually hanging on the wall.* "He kind of reminds me of you...around the eyes."

Philippe gazed over his shoulder at the painting. "I think he looks more like my younger brother, Chauncey."

"Shawn-see?" I tried to roll my tongue around the name and to pronounce it as he had. "I looked him up online. His crash was big news in racing circles."

Philippe made a non-committal sound in

reply, walked over, and sat beside me on the couch.

"How is your brother doing with his recovery?" I asked.

"He's doing a lot of physical therapy. According to my *grand-père* he's fairly miserable to be around at the moment."

"Oh." I scooped up some noodles. "Your brother lives with your grandpa in France? What about your parents?"

"Chauncey is staying with *grand-père* for the time being," Philippe said. "We share the same father, but have different mothers. Chauncey is my half brother."

"Are your parents divorced?"

Yes, my father and his second wife travel frequently, so Chauncey chose to stay with *grand-père*. Honestly, I don't think they are getting along very well."

Hearing his comment about his father and step-mother made me wonder about my own absent mother. I hadn't heard from her in over a year and had no idea what she was up to...probably still looking to land husband number four.

"Your brother is lucky to have a grandfather who cares," I said. "My parents were divorced too. After my father, Daniel, died my mother gave up custody of us to our grandmother."

"I did not know that." Philippe said.

"My sisters and I were very blessed to be raised by our Gran." I said, studying the remains of my soup. "I think I'm most nervous about her reaction when I tell the family about the baby."

"I will go with you." Philippe made it a statement, not an offer.

Unsure of how to respond, I slid my gaze over to the painting again. "Why don't you tell me about Pierre Michel Marquette? He looks like he has a story to tell."

"Pierre Michel was a rogue, the younger of the two brothers," Philippe said. "The oldest, my great-great-great grandfather, was Claude."

"Claude," I said, finishing my soup. "Did Claude have a painting?"

"It's displayed at the estate in France."

Displayed at the estate? I considered how casually he'd said that.

"The story goes that Claude was a dutiful

son," Philippe continued. "He married well and produced five sons."

"Five?" I asked, interrupting. "All boys?"

"*Oui*," Philippe smiled. "In my family there have been no daughters born for several generations."

"Oh boy," I said, placing a hand to my belly.

"I would guess that our baby is a boy," Philippe said gently, making me smile.

"The doctor told me, I could probably find out the gender around the 18-20 week mark," I said.

Philippe carefully added his hand on top of mine. "Did you want to find out the gender before the child is born?"

"Probably." I shrugged. "But it sounds like it's a good chance—"

"It will be a boy," Philippe finished.

"I guess we'll find out in six weeks or so." I nibbled on a cracker. "Tell me more about Claude and his brother, Pierre Michel."

"While Claude was an obedient son, Pierre Michel was more of a troublemaker. He enjoyed the company of, shall we say, more unsavory characters, than the polite society his parents would have preferred."

I leaned forward. "Ooh, like saloon girls and riverboat gamblers? That type of thing?" I could almost imagine it. "You know that Ames Crossing was quite the happening place in its heyday? It was a primary grain shipping port, and the railroad came right through the town."

Philippe smiled. "Yes, that's what my *grand-père* always told us. To get back to the story though, Pierre Michel's father had arranged an advantageous match with a local girl, and Pierre Michel refused—at first."

"Advantageous?" I sputtered. "An arranged marriage?"

"Gabriella," Philippe raised his eyebrows. "Are you going to let me tell you the tale or are your modern sensibilities going to be outraged with every other sentence?"

"I consider myself a feminist."

"I am not at all surprised," Philippe replied. "Please remember this was almost two hundred years ago...it truly was a different world then."

"Yeah, yeah." I gestured with a cracker. "Go on."

"Eventually Pierre Michel was brought to

heel, but barely a month after the wedding his new bride, Bridgette, disappeared—along with her dowry."

"Did they suspect foul play?" I asked.

"That's the thing, they never did find the girl. Her family was wealthy, connected—the girl's uncle had been a railroad baron, and an air of suspicion fell across Pierre Michel and the rest of the Marquette family."

"Her family thought that he'd taken the girl's dowry and bumped her off or something? What happened to Pierre Michel?" I wanted to know.

"No charges were brought against him, and he died six months later in a carriage accident."

"Wow." I studied the arrogant looking young man from the portrait. "And why is his portrait here?"

"It was uncovered last year during the first of the renovations," Philippe said.

"Uncovered?"

"It had been wrapped up and put inside of a wall. When we removed the wall during renovation, it was discovered, and I had the painting restored."

"Why was it hidden?" I asked around a

yawn.

"That..." Philippe smiled. "Is the mystery."

My eyes began to droop. Before I realized what he was intending, Philippe took the empty mug from me, and tucked my knees over his lap.

"That's some impressively gothic family history." I yawned hugely. "Cammy would love that."

"Get some rest, Gabriella." He patted my knee, and to my surprise I immediately fell asleep.

CHAPTER SIX

Morning came, and with it, reality. I woke up and eased into a sitting position on the couch. I sipped at the can of warm ginger ale that was still on a coaster from the night before. The light coming in through the windows was watery, and a lamp burned low across the room. Power must have been restored at some point during the night. As I sat there, I tried to work out what to do next.

"No more procrastinating," I muttered, and slowly reached for my phone. When the room didn't spin, I sent a text to my sisters and to Gran. Telling them I wanted to talk to them and asking them all to meet me at the farmhouse in an hour.

Philippe walked in with a small plate of

toast. "You look better," he said, and handed me a piece.

"Thanks," I said, and lowered the phone.

"Were you contacting your family?" Philippe guessed.

"Yes," I said, and reached for the toast. "I asked them to meet me at the farmhouse in an hour. I'm going to tell them all today." I burped. "About the baby."

He eased down beside me on the couch. "Gabriella, *we* will speak to your family today, together."

I balked. "That's not necessary."

"Yes," Philippe said, softly. "Yes, it is."

"Look, if you think you're going to swoop back into my life and take over..."

"*Ma belle*." He smiled. "There will be no 'swooping'. I am here now, and we are going to go through this pregnancy together."

I sighed. "I'm not expecting a relationship with you, Philippe."

"Oh?" He raised his eyebrows. "That's exactly what I was expecting out of you before I was called away to France."

"You were?" I said, around the toast.

"I was."

I thought about how best to respond to that, but wasn't sure. After I finished the toast I cleared my throat. "Would it be okay if I took a shower here?"

"Of course," he stood up and helped me to my feet. He waited, making sure I was steady and then he walked me to the bathroom. Normally, I would have swiped at him for the hovering, but I felt like hell. Philippe laid out a couple of towels for me and turned on the water, adjusting the temperature and spray.

"I can manage a shower all by myself," I grumbled, standing there in his t-shirt.

"That's the point, *ma belle*," he said seriously. "You don't have to manage by yourself, not any more. I'll be right outside if you need anything. Please call if you feel light headed."

"Thank you." I nodded and he went out, closing the door behind him.

About an hour later I pulled into the driveway behind the farmhouse. At his insistence, Philippe had ridden along with me.

"This hovering shit, is going to get old, real

quick." I warned him as I parked the car.

"You don't feel well, and are nervous." He half-smiled. "I'm going to let that comment go."

I scowled at him, grabbed my purse, and climbed out of the car. I started up the path through the back gardens and Philippe stayed at my side.

My bravado lasted until I hit the back porch and had to struggle to master the complex task of opening the door. I almost started to cry, and burped instead. "Goddess give me strength." I whispered, closing my eyes and trying to get ahold of myself.

"It will be alright," he murmured, and brushed a kiss across my hair. "They love you."

Suddenly glad I wasn't doing this alone after all, I walked into the kitchen with Philippe. My sisters and Gran fell silent when we came in together.

"Ella?" Drusilla frowned at the two of us. "What's going on?"

My knees were shaking hard and I went directly to the table to sit. Philippe came and stood behind my chair. "Can we all sit down?" I gestured to the empty chairs.

My sisters sat on either side of me and Gran took the chair on the opposite side of the table. She cast a considering stare at Philippe, but remained silent.

"So..." I began, "you've probably noticed I haven't been acting like myself lately."

"Are you sick?" Dru put her hand on my arm.

I felt Philippe's fingers rest on my back in encouragement. "No, I'm not sick. I'm pregnant," I blurted out.

"Shut the front door!" Cammy's jaw dropped. "*That's* why you've been acting all crabby and weird."

I laughed. "I believe what you meant to say was 'acting like a raging bitch'."

"Well, yeah." Cammy smirked. "But I was trying to be nice."

"How far along are you?" Gran asked. She was very calm, and it was a little scary.

"Nine weeks," I said, gulping as my stomach roiled.

"Is everything going well?" Dru asked gently.

"Besides the morning sickness?" I studied Dru's eyes, and all I saw was compassion. "Yeah, I'm okay."

"And who, may I ask, is the father?" Gran's stern tone of voice had me wincing.

Philippe rested his hand on my shoulder. "I'm the father."

"Whoa!" Cammy said, her eyes going huge.

"Have you been to the doctor?" Drusilla asked.

"Yes, I had my first ultrasound yesterday." Sweat started to roll down my back.

"Really?" Cammy did a happy dance in her seat. "Do you have pictures?"

"Yeah." I reached for my purse and pulled the photos out. Blindly, I passed one to Cammy and the other to Gran. *God, I felt awful!*

"Awww," Cammy said. "This is awesome!"

Drusilla leaned over and studied the picture with Gran. She was saying something but I couldn't quite hear her, instead there was this weird rushing sound.

"Ella!" Gran's voice was sharp.

"I'm sorry," I said, shaking my head, as black and white spots appeared in front of my eyes. "I think I need to lay down for a second..."

I opened my eyes and discovered that I was lying on the kitchen floor. My head was in someone's lap and I heard several excited voices all speaking at once. There was one that I latched on to. It was low, husky and had an accent.

"Philippe?" I looked around slowly.

"*Mon coeur*," he said. "I am taking you back to the doctor today."

"Why are you upside down?" I asked, confused.

"Because, your head is in his lap." That was from Cammy.

"The doctor says to bring her right in," Drusilla announced from somewhere off to the side.

"I'm okay," I said, and tried to believe it.

"Be quiet, Ella," Gran ordered.

"If I could just have a ginger ale," I said, weakly. "I'll be fine in a minute."

"Have you passed out before?" Drusilla wanted to know.

"No," I lied, as Philippe started to slowly

ease me upright.

"Yes," Philippe argued. "She fainted yesterday when she came to tell me."

"That's it." Gran stood and pointed to Philippe. "Put her in the car, young man."

"Now, let's not make a fuss," I argued, and was promptly ignored.

I was fine. I tried to tell them. But I found myself carried out to Drusilla's sedan by Philippe, and before I knew it I was sitting in the backseat between him and Cammy, with Dru driving and Gran riding shot gun.

Everyone piled in to the exam room with me as well. It was embarrassing, but they all insisted on it. My obstetrician took it in stride, shook Philippe's hand, and spoke to him calmly.

"I'm sorry about all this..." I tried to say over the questions my family fired at the doctor. I was told a combination of stress, not enough fluids, and fatigue was the reason behind the fainting spells. I sipped at a ginger ale, burped, and waited the family's multitude of questions out.

The doctor got out the fetal Doppler, I think

more to make Philippe feel better than anything, and the heartbeat of the baby was loud and clear.

Seeing the expressions on everyone's face was amazing as we listened. Cammy and Gran smiled. Dru got all misty, and Philippe took my hand and gave my fingers a squeeze. He sat very still for a moment, and then started to grin. Even with all the fuss from the family, I was glad he got to have that moment.

I was sent home and told to rest, eat small meals several times a day, push the fluids, and to avoid stress. Once we were back to the farmhouse Gran took me upstairs, helped me change into a night shirt and ordered me to bed.

Cammy and Drusilla came in with a few crackers and some water, and they both sat on the edge of my bed. A few minutes later Philippe poked his head in my room. "How are you feeling?" he asked.

I crossed my arms over my chest. "Embarrassed and tired." I burped. "Nauseous."

"You should ease up on the ginger ale," Dru suggested and patted my knee. "All those bubbles can't be helping with the burping."

I frowned. "I never thought of that."

Drusilla stood and tugged Cammy with her. "We'll leave the two of you alone."

"Thank you." Philippe inclined his head as my sisters left the room.

Cammy reached for the doorknob. "You two behave yourself in here." She tossed a wink and gently shut the door.

Alone with him, I wasn't sure where to begin. "I should apologize for all the fuss," I said.

"Is there anything I can get for you?" Philippe asked.

"A cure for morning sickness?" I blew out a long breath and leaned back against the pillows.

"The doctor told us that your stress was probably aggravating the symptoms."

I shut my eyes and stifled a yawn. "I know."

I felt the bed dip down as he sat beside me. "Do you mind if I sit with you for a while?" Philippe took my hand.

I cracked one eye open. "Not if you don't mind me falling asleep on you."

He lifted my hand and brushed a kiss over my fingers. "Get some rest," he suggested.

I rolled on my side toward him and linked my fingers with his. "You're being awfully nice to me. Probably nicer than I deserve."

"Why do you keep saying that?" He frowned.

"I don't know..." I yawned again, and was out like a light.

Thus began the hovering of the daughters of Midnight and Philippe Marquette. You know, most women would have probably been thrilled to have that much attention paid to them. But I was either perverse or the crabbiest pregnant woman on the planet, because the constant supervision and checking in was truly getting on my nerves.

I asked the family to keep the news between us for the time being, however I figured either Dru or Philippe would probably speak to Garrett. I tried to take that all in stride, because in a few months everyone would know anyway.

Cammy made copies of my ultrasound photos and had put the original ones in small frames. One was now sitting on my dresser, the other was on the mantle downstairs. She'd discreetly given a set of copies to Philippe, and it made me wish I'd have thought of that. She taped another set of copies to the refrigerator door. When I saw them there I started to cry, and Cammy had given me a hug and told me she hoped it would be a girl.

The mornings were still the worst. I thought I'd managed to ninja sneak my way to the bathroom a few days later, and was once again leaning over the toilet with my stomach heaving but still could not manage to actually throw up. It was horrible.

I whimpered in self-pity, and when the bathroom door opened I was too miserable to snarl at whoever had burst in. I heard the water running and the next thing I knew, a cold washcloth was held to the back of my neck.

"Oh sweetie," Drusilla said.

"Someone shoot me now." My voice echoed out of the toilet bowl.

I felt Dru gently pull my hair back and secure it away from my face. She stayed sitting on the bathroom rug with me until I finally leaned back. "Do you think you can get up?" she asked.

Feeling like the biggest wimp on the planet, I leaned my head on her shoulder. "Maybe, I'll sit here for the rest of my life."

Dru shifted the cold washcloth to my forehead. "Come on, let me help you." She looped an arm under my shoulders and eased me to my feet. I staggered my way across the hall to my room and suffered through the indignity of my sister insisting on helping me get dressed.

"I can do it," I said, hooking my bra into place.

"Ella, don't be so stubborn," Dru said, tugging a t-shirt over my head. "You are this ghastly shade of pale green at the moment."

I tugged on a pair of denim shorts and was surprised to discover they were snug at my waist. I tugged them down and sat on my bed to take them the rest of the way off.

"Here," Dru said, handing me a pair of old ratty gym shorts. "I bet these will be more comfortable."

I pulled them on. "Huh. I guess I'll need to get a few pairs of bigger shorts." I picked up the tumbled stones from the nightstand and dropped them in my pocket.

I made my way downstairs for some toast

and discovered that Gran had a surprise for me. Homemade brown lollipops were resting on a piece of parchment paper in the middle of the kitchen table.

"Try this." She peeled one off the paper. "It's ginger and mint flavored and will help your stomach."

Cautiously, I tasted one. It wasn't bad. "What's in these?" I asked.

"Apple cider vinegar, honey, mint and ginger." Gran answered.

"Hmm," I said. At least the flavor didn't make my nausea worse.

"I wish you would have told me sooner about the morning sickness." Gran ran a hand down my hair. "You shouldn't have had to suffer like this."

The house phone rang and Gran moved to answer it. "Good morning Garrett," she said.

Oh shit, I suddenly remembered. "I have a meeting with Garrett and Nicole today."

"I'll drive you over to Garrett's house," Dru volunteered.

I pulled the lollipop from my mouth. "Jeez, I'm not an invalid. I can drive myself."

Drusilla leaned over and got up in my face. "When you've gone a week without passing out on us, *then* you can drive your car again. Until that time, you can just suck it up, Buttercup."

"I—" When Dru narrowed her eyes at me, I reconsidered my argument and put the candy back in my mouth. "Fine. Okay," I mumbled around the candy.

Gran passed the phone to Dru, and she came and sat beside me. "If you feel up to it, you can try some chicken broth this morning," Gran said. "You need something in your belly besides water and toast."

"Yes ma'am," I said around the candy.

I sat there sucking on a lollipop and felt slightly ridiculous. But damned if the candy didn't actually help. Leave it to my Gran to pull an old wise woman's trick out of the bag.

***

That afternoon we pulled up in front of the brick Italianate house, and Dru put the car in park. "Do you want me to walk you in?" she asked kindly.

I gritted my teeth and reminded myself to be civil. "No thanks," I said, opening the car door. "I'm good." I stepped out of the car into the brutal August afternoon heat and acted like everything was absolutely fine.

Dru rolled down a window. "Call when you want a ride home." She smiled, and with a wave, backed out of the driveway.

I hitched my laptop carrier higher on my shoulder and hustled to the shady side of the house. Nervously, I checked my appearance in the reflection of the kitchen window. I was still a tad pale, but I'd been careful with the cosmetics and had managed to conceal most of the circles under my eyes. My long hair was twisted up and clipped off the back of my neck in an effort to remain as cool as possible. The sky-blue summer maxi dress I wore was comfortable at least. The empire waist made it feel flowing and light. I wiggled my toes in my flat leather sandals and knocked on the back door.

"Hi Ella!" Brooke pulled the door open and I ducked into the coolness of the house.

The jolt between the heat and the air

conditioning made my head spin slightly, but I walked directly to the table. Gripping the back of a wooden kitchen chair I eased myself down, waiting for the dizziness to pass.

Brooke was leaning over the table and peering at my face. "You look funny," she said.

"Oh yeah?" I said, pulling a horrible face that made the girl burst out laughing.

"Hi, Ella." Garrett's voice came from across the kitchen.

I cautiously rotated my head. I'd finally figured out that any sudden movements made me feel light headed. And as soon as I saw his face, it was obvious. *Yup,* I thought. *He knows.*

He smiled and detoured to the fridge. Garrett plucked a bottle of water out and brought it over to me. "How are you feeling today?" he asked courteously.

"Peachy keen, jelly bean," I answered.

Brooke made a comment about answering the doorbell and raced out of the room. I twisted the cap from the water bottle and took a sip.

"Philippe called me a couple of days ago," he said quietly.

"I figured as much." I slid my laptop from the carrier and booted it up.

He rested a kind hand on my shoulder. "I'm sorry that your morning sickness is bad."

I met his eyes. "Me too."

Anything else that might have been said came to an abrupt halt as Nicole Craig strolled in the kitchen. "Hello!" she said. "Brooke let me in."

"Hello, Nicole." Garrett smiled in greeting.

Today she was in a skin tight, navy blue dress. Of course, she looked amazing. Hair expertly styled, and her makeup flawless, she pressed an air kiss to Garrett's cheek. I frowned at her. In contrast, I sat there in a twenty dollar dress from Target and felt fat and frumpy.

I drank my water and waved at her in lieu of a greeting. Goddess only knew what would come out of my mouth. I had a tenuous grip on my filter these days, it was probably safest for me to keep my mouth shut.

"It sure is hot outside, isn't it?" she said, taking a seat at the farmhouse table. "You were smart to wear a loose, comfortable old dress today, Gabriella."

Old dress? Was that a put down? I wondered as she chatted away. I tilted my head to the side and watched her like a hawk, waiting to see what else she would say. Nicole pushed a rustic wooden bowl filled with apples out of the way to arrange her files on the table, chatting easily with Garrett.

Brooke returned to the kitchen with her kitten trailing behind her. While Nicole monopolized the conversation, I watched Brooke pull a popsicle out of the freezer. My stomach decided at that moment to gurgle, loudly.

"Sorry," I said, pressing a hand to it.

Brooke giggled over the sound. "Did you want a popsicle, Ella?" she asked.

I shrugged. "What flavor?"

"They're chocolate."

"*Yes!*" I heard my own reply and realized it sounded a little intense, but I didn't care. All I knew was I wanted a god-damn chocolate popsicle.

Brooke carried one over to me. I ripped the paper away and immediately bit in.

"Wow," Brooke said. "You weren't kidding

about wanting one."

"Oh. My. God." I sat back with an orgasmic sigh. "This tastes *good*." I took a second bite. I swallowed, took another greedy bite, and then another.

"Well," Nicole said, hesitantly. "I suppose we can wait while you finish that..."

Garrett cleared his throat as I proceeded to scarf down the fudgesicle. "Would you like another one, Ella?" he asked.

"*Really*?" I asked as I finished the first one. "You have more?"

In answer, Garrett rose to his feet and got it himself. He tore the paper off as he crossed the kitchen floor. "Enjoy," he said, holding it out.

I dropped the clean popsicle stick on the table top and snatched the second frozen chocolate treat from him.

Garrett frowned down at his hand. "Well that's a relief," he said, counting his fingers. "They're all still there."

"Ha!" I said, and kept right on eating. For the first time in months, something actually tasted good, and didn't make me feel sick. *It was heaven.* I sat back with a happy hum and devoured the second popsicle while they all waited. When it was finished, I took a swig of the water and did my best to squelch down a burp.

"Well, goodness," Nicole said, looking unsure. That pause only lasted a moment though. She took a breath and launched into her speech about the website.

CHAPTER SEVEN

While she droned on and on, I took notes and hoped to be able to ask a few pertinent questions. Eventually.

The damn woman wouldn't stop yapping. Lifting a hand to my hair, I tucked a wayward tendril behind my ear and checked the time on the clock that hung on the kitchen wall. Twenty-five minutes and counting. *Surely she would wind down, or stop and take a breath,* I thought. *Perhaps she'd die from a lack of oxygen*—I was good with any of those outcomes.

Mentally waving goodbye to my filter, I leaned forward and cut her off. "Thank you, Nicole, for that fascinating monologue."

Garrett barked out a laugh and tried to cover

it up with a cough.

"Excuse me?" Nicole's eyes grew wide in her face.

"Listen, I get it," I said. "You do PR. But for the love of god, shut up for a minute and let me ask a few questions, will ya?"

The kitchen door opened and Philippe walked in. He took in Nicole's shocked expression, and Garrett, who had dropped his head helplessly in his hands.

"What have I missed?" Philippe asked.

Nicole fluttered her eyelashes and flashed a mega-watt smile at Philippe. "We seem to be having a slight miscommunication at the moment." She focused on me and continued. "Gabriella." Her voice was saccharine-sweet. "Perhaps you simply don't grasp the intricacies of Public Relations."

"Nicole, grasp *this*," I shot back. "Your whole fake, uber chipper attitude makes me want to beat you to death with your own designer shoes."

"Oh, snap," Brooke said, starting to laugh.

Nicole gasped, pressing a hand to her throat, and I heard Philippe mutter something in

French.

"What in the world is wrong with you?" Nicole asked me.

"My bullshit barometer is at an all time low these days." A burp escaped. "Oops." I pressed my fingers to my lips a tad too late. "Excuse me."

"For the love of god." Garrett's shoulders were shaking.

"I've never seen you like this, Ella," Nicole said.

"Pregnancy is a bitch," I said, and flinched, remembering too late that Brooke was standing right there.

"Oh my god!" Brooke said. "Are you having a *baby*?"

I faced the girl. "Yes, I am."

She raced to me with a happy squeal and threw her arms around my shoulders.

"*We* are having a baby," Philippe corrected.

Brooke jerked back and her eyes went from mine to Philippe's. "You and Uncle Philippe made a baby?"

I flushed at the way she put it. "Surprise," I managed, with a weak laugh.

I saw Nicole's shocked expression over Brooke's shoulder. It lasted about two seconds, and then I could swear I saw the gears starting to turn in the publicist's head.

"When are you due?" Brooke demanded.

"In the month of March," I said.

"This is the coolest thing *ever*!" Brooke announced. She let me go and ran to throw her arms around Philippe.

"You'll have an honorary cousin next year, *cherie*," Philippe said, pressing a kiss to the top of her bright red hair.

"Congratulations to you both." Nicole gave us a polite smile. "Perhaps we can pick up this meeting at a later date when Gabriella is feeling better." She gathered up her files and purse from the table, nodded to the men, excused herself, and left.

The room was silent until the sound of the front door closing carried back to the kitchen.

Garrett leaned back with a groan and scrubbed his hands over his face. "I think we may have lost our Public Relations person."

Philippe narrowed his eyes at me.

"Aw come on!" I pointed at Garrett. "Tell me

you haven't been sitting there for the past half hour, trying to figure out a way to shut her up."

"I was," Brooke chimed in. "I don't like Nicole at all. She does all those fake, air kissy things."

"*Faire la bise*," Philippe corrected.

"Leave it to the Frenchman." I rolled my eyes. "Of course you'd know that."

"You're going to need to apologize to Nicole," Garrett warned me.

"No, I won't." I shrugged. "She'll get over it."

Garrett pointed at me. "You threatened to beat her to death—"

"*With her own designer shoes*!" Brooke burst out laughing. "That was awesome, Ella!"

"*Merde*." Philippe tipped his head up and stared at the ceiling.

I glanced at Philippe. "Doesn't that word mean, *shit*?"

"Exactly." Brooke nodded enthusiastically. "Philippe told me some other French swear words, Ella. If you want, I'll teach you some."

"Deal," I said to the girl, making her laugh again.

"Brooke!" Garrett frowned at the girl.

"Gabriella." Philippe rested his hand on my shoulder. "What exactly have you done to poor Nicole?"

"Poor Nicole?" I scowled at him, and then at Garrett for good measure. "For gods sake, you two! She and her ego will be *fine*. Besides, she has Max to comfort her."

I saw Philippe frown over my comment, but I was distracted when Brooke went to the fridge. "Do you want another popsicle, Ella?" she asked.

"Hell, yeah." I made a come ahead gesture.

"How many of those has she had?" Philippe asked.

"Two," Garrett said.

"It's a fudgesicle you guys," I pointed out. "Not an illegal substance."

"You should be more careful with your diet, *ma belle*," Philippe said. He picked up an apple from the bowl on the table. "Try this instead."

Suspiciously, I sniffed the apple he'd handed me and waited for my stomach to revolt. When it didn't I took a cautious bite. "Oh, wow." I said with my mouth full. "This tastes good too."

Philippe sat in the chair next to me. "When you've finished your snack, I'd like you to show me the changes to the winery website."

I nodded and devoured the apple, relieved and happy to have found *anything* that sat well on my stomach.

Apples and fudgesicles... I thought. *Who knew?*

***

It was only a matter of time before Max heard about my pregnancy, word would travel down the grapevine soon enough. I imagined Nicole had run directly to Max that day to cry on his shoulder.

I held my breath for a while, half expecting Max to want to talk to me, but I didn't see him. Thankfully, the morning sickness finally began to ease up. I don't know if it was from being further along, the fact that my stress had been reduced now that the family knew, if it was because Philippe was back, or perhaps it was the anti-nausea lollipops my Gran had made. Maybe it was a combination of all of it.

Philippe started dropping by the house almost every day, and he kept me stocked up on apples and fudgesicles. He gently encouraged me to take walks in the morning when it was cooler, that way I wasn't sitting at my computer desk all day. It was a good idea, and since I wasn't hanging over the toilet dry heaving anymore, I was open to the idea of walking with him. It wasn't exactly a hardship...spending time with an attractive and attentive man.

Once a week he brought me flowers: blue hydrangeas, cheerful golden sunflowers next, and recently, white Shasta daisies. In the language of flowers he'd given me: devotion, adoration, and patience. All of the flowers he'd brought were unscented too. I had to give the man props for noticing that strong fragrances bothered me. He was romantic and thoughtful, and if I was honest, I was beginning to fall for the good-looking Frenchman.

He took me on a picnic one nice evening. We ate roasted chicken at a park alongside of the river and sipped sparkling apple juice. He told me about the grape harvest, and it was fascinating. Which made me I wonder if I could get some photos and add a section to the website about the wine making process. We discussed my idea, and Philippe was, as ever, charming and easy company.

I looked forward to spending time with him everyday, and interestingly, he never pushed for a physical aspect to our 'relationship'. Not that he wasn't romantic, but other than kisses, and holding my hand, things were pretty tame. It confused the hell out of me, and I wasn't sure what to make of him. Gran said he was courting me, and I found that idea ridiculous considering everything.

It was more likely he was simply being nice to me since I was carrying his child. Either that or he was trying to keep me happy so I wouldn't upset any other winery employees. Garrett must have smoothed things over with Nicole. She was still the PR person for the winery, and from what I heard she and Max were still a couple.

The heat finally broke in September. I started my second trimester and was faced with the reality of wearing maternity clothes. I ordered some things online, and then had to rearrange my dresser and closet to make room for them. That's how I found the spell I'd written for the night of the masquerade party.

"Oh, hello," I murmured, holding the paper up to the light of the afternoon sun. Suddenly the reality of exactly what I'd cast for hit me like a ton of bricks. My knees went to jello and I quickly sat on the hope chest at the end of my bed.

"With these words I now weave a charm so true..." I cautiously read the spell out loud. "Glamour bound to a mask of midnight blue. May this spell catch his eye and bolster my heart; a confidence spell cast with a wise woman's art. Let him finally see me as I wish to be seen; a desirable woman, and not merely a dream. No longer his friend, but a lover both brave and bold, may a new life begin from the ashes of the old."

Shadow hopped beside me and swatted at the page that I held. The room started to spin, and I carefully eased down to carpet on the floor. My heart began to race and I broke a sweat while the implications of that verse began to sink in.

I stayed with my back leaning against the trunk for a few minutes and breathed my way through the panic attack. My eyes zeroed in on the final line of the spell. *May a new life begin from the ashes of the old.* I gulped. "Oh, holy shit." I curled one hand protectively over my belly.

"A new *life*," I whispered, dropping the paper to the floor. "By the moon and stars, what have I done?"

"Knock, knock," Cammy called out, and opened the door to my room. "Hey!" she raced to me on the floor. "Ella, are you okay?"

"I think I'm having a panic attack." I blew out a long breath.

"Do you want me to call Gran?" Cammy took my hand. "You're as white as a ghost."

"No," I said, gripping her fingers. "But I'm going to need *your* help Cammy."

"My help?" Cammy frowned at me. "What's wrong?"

"I need some advice," I said, leaning back. "Magickal advice."

Cammy raised an eyebrow.

"Do me a favor," I said. "Shut the door, I

want to keep this between you and me."

Cammy got up and did what I asked. "What is going on?"

I eyeballed her and noticed with a start that she was wearing a gray t-shirt that proclaimed, *Resting Witch Face.* "Did you wear that shirt to work at the winery?" I asked.

"Yeah, I did." Cammy plunked her hands on her hips. "People loved it."

"Real subtle, Sis."

"You're changing the subject and trying to stall." She raised an eyebrow at me. "I can see through your Jedi mind tricks. What's up?"

I held out the spell. "I worked this spell on the night of the masquerade party, with the intention to give myself courage to tell Max that I loved him."

Cammy took the paper and sat beside me. "Let me see..." She read it silently and when she finished, her eyes met mine over the page. "First question. Did you use this *exact* wording or did you say anyone's name out loud?"

I rubbed my hands over my face. "I chanted it exactly as it was written, and I swear to you I did *not* intentionally target anyone."

"The wording of the spell is pretty vague," Cammy said. "I get that your intention was to bolster your courage. But, damn it, Gabriella! You cast a glamour? You know better."

I cringed at her tone. "I did put all the magick into the mask, not on anybody specifically—other than myself."

"Start at the beginning, from when you cast the spell," Cammy urged me. "Tell me everything that happened that night." She went to my desk, grabbed a notebook and a pencil. "Both with Max and Philippe. Don't leave anything out."

I took a breath, squared my shoulders and confided in my younger sister. I didn't leave anything out.

"I'll say this for you." Cammy rubbed a hand across my shoulders. "You ticked every damn box with that spell. You caught both Max and Philippe's eye, and did bolster your confidence that night. You took a lover and became brave and bold."

"What if Philippe's feelings were manipulated somehow by the magick?" I asked her.

Cammy thought that over. "I was there that night. He spotted you the moment we arrived."

"That's right," I remembered. "He walked directly to me before I even had the chance to speak to Max."

"Obviously the spell didn't affect Max the same way." Cammy tapped the pencil against her lips. "He might have been enchanted by a mystery woman, but when Max realized that it was you, he was—"

"Horrified," I finished for her. "He was horrified, as soon as he discovered that it was me behind the mask."

"Max thinks of you like a sister, and once he saw you, the magick had no more influence over him."

"Okay." I faced Cammy. "I'm starting to get where you're going with this."

"Now, when it came to bachelor number two..." She wiggled her eyebrows. "Philippe obviously saw you as a desirable woman, and he became your lover."

"Philippe did take the mask off my face *before* we made love," I said. "If that was the breaking point for Max, do you think it's possible that Philippe wasn't under the influence of the glamour after that moment in time?"

"Possibly...but the magick still worked almost exactly as you requested." Cammy patted my belly. "Because here's the 'new life from the ashes of old'."

Silently, I raised my eyes to hers.

"Be careful what you wish for," Cammy said, gently.

"Cammy, I'm worried. What if Philippe's current feelings toward me are still being swayed by the spell?"

"What do you mean?" she asked, tucking the pencil in the notebook.

"Philippe's been wonderful. Why else would he be so damn thoughtful, sweet, caring and considerate to me if he wasn't spellbound? I'm an average woman. His one-time hook-up that got pregnant. And he's freaking gorgeous. What is a man like that doing with me?"

"I think you're underestimating yourself," Cammy argued.

"But what if I'm right, and Philippe's still under the influence of the glamour?"

"I suppose there's only one way to find out." Cammy ran a hand through her pink hair. "Where the hell is that mask now?"

I blanched. "I don't know." I dropped my head between my knees.

"Where was the last place you saw it?"

"In the Marquette mansion the night of the party. That was more than three months ago. Goddess knows where it is now."

"My intuition tells me it's still in the mansion," Cammy said. "You need to get your happy ass up there and search for it. Destroy the mask and be absolutely sure that the spell is broken."

"Alright." I nodded. "In the mean time I'd feel better if I started working to minimize any —*if* there are any—emotional side effects of that spell. Realizing how it misled Max, and that it may still be inadvertently manipulating Philippe's reactions, makes me feel sick."

"I can help you put something together," Cammy said.

"I'll take whatever help I can get."

Cammy got Gran out of the house a few hours later. Dru was on a date with Garrett, leaving me alone, for once. I waited until twilight as the in-between time would be best for working to nix any effects of the glamour. As the crickets sang in the back gardens I gathered a few zinnia flowers and a dozen rose pink petals from the roses growing around the gazebo.

I set up a work area by the fire pit on a small side table. Snipping off a head of blooming blue hydrangea, I crumbled the blossoms into the wooden bowl on top of the rose petals. I'd chosen those specific flowers to work with as we had them on hand, and hydrangeas were good for breaking negative spells. The rose petals would speed up the effects of the neutralizing magick I was casting tonight.

The zinnias I crumbled in my hands and scattered their petals in a circle around my work area. "With these fragrant petals, a circle I now cast," I chanted, walking the circumference of the ritual space. "Create for me a sacred space and good magick that will last." In the language of flowers, the zinnias spoke of *absent friends*, and I thought the symbolism appropriate.

With Shadow staying by my side like the

loyal familiar he was, I lit a white candle and dropped it down inside of a glass votive holder to protect it from any breezes. The night was calm fortunately, and I pulled that original spell from the pocket of my casual dress, carefully unfolding it. I placed the spell in the bottom of the fire pit, took a deep, calming breath, and began.

"By the power of the waxing moon; I now end any ill effects from the glamour that I cast in June," I said. "A love conjured is a false love and so it must fade away; any magick that influenced Philippe Marquette is neutralized today."

"By the powers of earth." I tossed a handful of hydrangea petals in the pit. "By air, fire and water; goddess hear the call of your daughter." I picked up the lighter, held the flame to the edge of the original spell paper, and continued with the verse. "Philippe Marquette you are now free from my magick. As the paper burns away; any influence will now fade. Hydrangea breaks hexes and negativity; may these petals halt any enchantment between you and me."

I struggled not to cry as the spell components

began to burn. Of course I'd hoped that Philippe actually desired and cared for me naturally—all on his own. My breath caught when the paper and petals flared with a paranormally bright orange flame. A sure sign that the spell was being broken.

The flames went out, sending smoke curling up from the fire pit. It hovered for a moment in front of me, and then a gust of wind rushed through the garden. It was strong enough to send the skirt of my pink midi dress snapping. The circle of zinnia petals blew away, across my bare feet and out and over the lawn. Taking advantage of the boost from the elements, I quickly grabbed the flower filled bowl.

"May the element of air strengthen my work!" I tossed the contents up in the air and the petals were caught in the wind. "Be free Philippe, your path is your own to choose." As I spoke the petals swirled and spun up into the air and were swept away. Shocked at seeing a spell manifest in such a dramatic fashion, I eased down to one knee on the brick pavers.

"As I will it. So mote it be." I managed to close up the spell as my personal energy level dropped.

I stayed there for a couple of moments and shakily rose to my feet. Shadow leaned against my leg in support. I wiped away a few tears that had fallen and reminded myself that self-pity was unattractive.

"It's for the best, Shadow," I said. "Because if I did manipulate that gorgeous Frenchman in any way with magick, then I truly don't deserve him."

"Meow," Shadow chimed in.

Taking my time to clean up the spell components, I placed the candle and votive holder inside the fire pit where it could safely finish burning. Shadow scampered to the back porch and sat, waiting for me.

Satisfied that I'd done everything I could for the moment, I picked up the now-empty bowl and started for the farmhouse. The sound of a racing car had me freezing in place. I turned my head and watched as a pickup truck came screeching to a halt in the back driveway. Max Dubois hopped out and slammed his truck door closed.

"Gabriella!" he shouted. "I want a word with

you!"

I braced myself. The magick had definitely begun to work. The man I'd thought I'd loved, and the reason I'd tried the spell in the first place, marched over to me. A friend, absent no longer.

CHAPTER EIGHT

Max's gaze raked me up and down, taking in the loose-fitting dress. "Nicole finally told me," he said.

"I'm frankly surprised that she stayed silent about it for the past three weeks," I said.

"I couldn't believe it!" Max got right up in my face. "You're pregnant and *Marquette* is the father?"

I held my ground as he towered over me. "That's correct." I kept my voice even.

"How did this happen?" Max demanded.

"Jeez, Max." Despite myself, I started to laugh. "Even you should know the answer to that."

"*When* did this happen?"

He wasn't going to like my answer. I set the

bowl aside, folded my arms over my middle, and braced myself for his reaction. "The night of the masquerade."

"That son of a bitch!" Max snarled. "I'm going to kick his ass."

"Why?" I tossed my head. "You made it abundantly clear that you didn't have romantic feelings for me. Why should it matter?"

"Because it just does!"

"You can't have it both ways, Max." I tried to keep my voice down and to maintain a grip on my own temper. "You can't *not* want me and turn around and be pissed that someone else actually does."

"No, that's not what I meant," he said. "You were in a vulnerable emotional state that night! That man took advantage of you."

"The fuck he did!" I shot back.

"Ella!" Max chastised me. "Watch your language."

"Philippe did *not* take advantage of me!" I argued. "If anything, *I* took advantage of an opportunity that presented itself. An attractive man found me desirable, made me feel beautiful and sexy...and I acted on it."

"And look where that got you!" Max tossed up his hands. "Now you're going to have to deal with the mistake you made."

I smacked him on the arm. "This baby is *not* a mistake. How dare you say so!"

"Exactly what are you telling me? Did you plan all of this?"

"No, I didn't," I said. "Not intentionally."

"What does that even mean?" Max's mouth dropped open. "You weren't playing around with magick, were you?"

I glared at him. "I take great personal offense at the term, 'playing around'."

"I know you." Max gentled his voice. "In my mind we're family. I know when you're lying, and I'm familiar with every expression on your face."

"You didn't recognize me the night of the masquerade," I pointed out.

"And was there any magick in play that night?"

I turned my face away instead of answering.

"You look guilty as hell, right about now, Ella."

"Fine!" I snapped. "I may have had a slight

magickal snafu, and it might have influenced how things ultimately ended up...but that doesn't matter any more."

"Oh shit." Max sounded horrified. "What did you do?"

"I'm not getting into the particulars with you," I said. "The fact is that I am doing my best to fix whatever went wrong with the spell." In my anger, a couple of tears spilled over.

Max glanced around the yard. "It feels different out here. Were you casting?"

"I told you, I worked to minimize any damage I may have caused." My voice broke and my knees started to shake.

Max immediately put an arm around me. "Hey, are you alright?" he asked.

"By the goddess, I'm tired," I said, honestly.

"You should sit down." Max herded me over to sit on the big blue wooden bench in the garden. "You're not going to faint or anything, are you? Nicole said you've been really sick."

"The nausea is mostly over these days."

"Why are you so pale?" Max asked.

"I'm a little wiped out. When you cast a big spell, it can be draining." I blew out a breath and tried to ground my energy.

"Maybe you should be careful with that spell-casting stuff right now."

"I'm fine. I promise."

He took my hand and gave my fingers a squeeze. "Are we done shouting at each other?"

"Maybe." I sniffled. "I could yell at you some more, if you'd like."

One side of his mouth curved up. "I've missed you, Ella. You've been my best friend for years."

"I missed you too," I said, and tried to *act* like a decent friend. "Are you happy..." I was careful with my tone, "with Nicole back in your life?"

"I am." Max's voice was quiet, but sincere.

"How about you?" he asked. "Are you happy with Marquette?"

"It's complicated," I admitted.

"How so?"

"I'm scared, Max. Scared that I could lose Philippe." I leaned my head against Max's broad shoulder. "Especially after the work I did tonight."

"Don't be afraid," he said. "You're not alone.

I'll always be here if you need anything."

"Cut that out." I struggled to keep my emotions in check. "You're going to make me cry."

"I love you, Ella," he said softly. "You're like the sister I never had." Max tipped his head over and rested it on top of mine. "Listen, if you need someone to be your labor coach, or to help you figure out how to install a baby car seat...I'll be there for you."

"I know you will." I sighed. "Damn it. I love you too, Max."

"Is Marquette going to do the right thing by you?" Max wanted to know.

I scoffed at that. "What century are we living in? What's that supposed to even mean?"

Max tipped my chin up to meet his eyes. "I meant, is he going to marry you?"

"Marry?" I blanched, and could literally feel the blood drain from my face. "I honestly don't think that will happen."

"Ella," Max's voice was gentle. "The child deserves a father."

"And he has one," Philippe's voice came unexpectedly from the left.

"Philippe?" My breath came out in a horrified squeak.

"*Oui*." Philippe said, glaring at me and Max.

How long had Philippe been here? I wondered frantically. *How much had he overheard?*

"Marquette," Max growled. "I want a few words with you."

"At your service." Philippe saluted Max. "But first, take your hands off the mother of my child."

Max stood up and began to stalk toward Philippe.

They were going to beat the crap out of each other, I realized with no small amount of horror. Before blows could fall, I jumped up and raced to get between them. "Don't you dare hit him!" I said.

Philippe stopped in his tracks. "Are you speaking to him, or to me?"

"To both of you Neanderthals!" I snapped.

"Back off," Philippe said to Max, stepping forward.

"I'm not leaving," Max tossed back.

"Stop it!" I slapped a hand to each of their

chests, and a jolt of power transferred out. It wasn't entirely pleasant. Like a nasty snap of static electricity from the palm of my hands and into the center of both the men's chests, it made me gasp in pain. "Ouch!" I immediately yanked my hands back away from the two of them.

Philippe flinched. "What was that?"

"Damn it, Ella!" Max winced and rubbed the heel of his hand over his chest. "Did you just zap me with your witchcraft?"

"Sorry," I said, shaking my fingers out.

"Did you say, *witchcraft*?" Philippe asked.

"Shit, she didn't tell you?" Max rolled his eyes to the heavens.

"I never had the chance." I swatted Max's arm. "Thanks for outing me like that. Real smooth."

"Sorry." Max shrugged.

I turned my attention completely to Philippe, who stood staring at me like I had two heads. "Technically," I began, "I don't consider myself a Witch, per se."

Philippe's response was to lower his brow, tilt his head, and narrow his eyes suspiciously.

I scrambled to explain, before he jumped to

an inaccurate conclusion. "The women of my family are descended from healers and herbalists. It's a path of wisdom often misunderstood."

"*Sorcières.*" Philippe's voice was soft and considering.

I knew very few French words, but I knew that one translated to: witches. "We prefer the term, *wise women.*" I corrected him automatically.

"*Une femme sage,*" Philippe said, studying me. "I am familiar with the term, and Max, he knew?"

"We've been best friends for years." Max rested a supportive hand on my shoulder. "Of course I knew."

"I won't tell you again, Dubois, keep your hands to yourself." Philippe growled and pulled me away from Max.

Max shifted his weight as if he was going to throw a punch at Philippe. "Max, don't!" I said.

I not sure what would have happened next, but to my utter shock Nicole waltzed into the back gardens from around the front of the house. "Alright gentleman." Her voice carried clearly. "This caveman type of behavior certainly isn't helping the situation."

"Nicole?" I said, feeling like my eyes were going to pop out of my head.

She gave me a cheerful wink and waded right in the middle of things. "Max, you need to calm down," she said taking ahold of his arm.

"Stay out of this," Max said to her. "He's got it coming for—"

"Honey," she cut him off. "I know you're concerned for Gabriella, but this is *not* the way to handle things."

"Babe, please give me a—" Max began.

She slid her hand down and took his fingers in hers. "You've said your piece. Now I think we need to give Philippe and Gabriella some privacy." Her gaze shifted from my face to Philippe's. "I have a hunch they need to talk a few things out."

"*Merci*, Nicole." Philippe inclined his head, thanking the brunette.

"*Bien sûr*," she replied, and tugged Max back a few steps.

"What does that mean?" I asked suspiciously.

"It means, 'of course'." She smiled. "You

two have a nice evening." And with that she and Max exited toward the front of the house.

"I hadn't even heard her drive up," I said, watching them leave.

"We arrived together," Philippe said, blowing out a long breath.

"You did?" I asked.

He slid one finger under my chin and tipped my face up to his. "You and I, we need to have a long talk."

I studied his face. "You probably have some questions about my family's practices."

"We'll get to that," he said. "For now, I want some privacy." Philippe gently took me by the elbow and started to walk me across the back yard. "Come with me."

"No one's home," I said. "We can talk right here."

"No," he said, and continued to steer me along.

"What do you mean, *no*?" I yanked away from him and lost my balance. I put a hand on the side of the house for support.

"Are you feeling unwell?" he asked.

That last spell took it out of me, I thought,

but didn't think he'd appreciate the humor. "I'm tired," I said instead.

He solved the problem by scooping me up.

"Put me down, Philippe," I ordered.

He hitched me up higher in his arms and my breath caught. "There, that made you quiet." He smirked and carted me to the front driveway, where he put me in the passenger seat of his car.

I'd resisted the urge to snuggle closer while I'd been in his arms and tried instead to figure out exactly how I would explain everything to him. When he reached for the seatbelt though, I batted his hands away. "Jeez, I can do it myself. I'm not a child."

"Then don't act like one," he suggested.

While I sat there gaping at him, he strolled around the hood and slid in the driver's seat.

"Now sit still and behave yourself," he suggested. "If you are able."

I whipped my head around. "I don't know what has gotten into you..." I began.

"You are about to find out, *ma belle*."

I sat and considered the sudden change in his attitude. *The neutralizing spell was obviously working,* I realized. *Which would mean that the sweet, considerate man who'd been pampering me for the past few weeks was probably gone for good.*

The trip to Notch Cliff was short, and I ran through a half dozen scenarios in my mind on how I would apologize for the magickal mistake. *How much had he overheard of my conversation with Max? Could I even make him understand a wise woman's traditions? What if magick freaked him out?* Back and forth my mind went, and I was so nervous that I bolted from the car before Philippe had barely put it into park.

Catching myself, I took a deep breath and connected to the solid and stable vibrations of the earth. I squelched down my panic, shut my eyes, and planted my bare feet. Visualizing the drawing up of natural energy from the earth, I slowed my breathing and grounded my personal power. When I opened my eyes, I found that Philippe was standing silently, watching me.

"I'll be happy to answer any questions you may have," I said, trying to sound as calm and reasonable as possible.

He shut the car door and considered me. "Be assured, you will, Gabriella." His serious tone was intimidating. However, he walked to the door, pushed it open, and stood holding it for me.

I psyched myself up and went inside. Refusing to follow him like some meek little mouse, I strode up the stairs to the refurbished wing that he lived in. I went straight to the tower room and took a seat on the couch.

Philippe followed at a more sedate pace and when he closed the door behind him, I tried not to flinch.

"Relax, Gabriella," he said, studying me from across the room. "I'm not going to jump you."

I scoffed. "I'd like to see you try." The slow look he sent my way had me immediately regretting that particular verbal bluff. I crossed my arms over my chest. "Well, whatever is on your mind, let's hear it."

Philippe crossed the room and stood by the mantle. Seeing him stand beneath the portrait of his ancestor reminded me all over again how different the two of us were. How dissimilar our upbringing and lifestyle truly was.

"I held my tongue while you were feeling so unwell," he said. "I've been patient, giving you both time and some breathing room...but now Gabriella, you are going to listen to me."

About a half-dozen pithy responses to that order sprang to mind. But I bit my tongue and tried to be magnanimous. "I'm listening."

"You will stay away from Max Dubois."

My jaw dropped. "What?"

"If you have fears or worries about our child, you will share them with me, *not* him."

"Well, I—"

"The *only* labor coach in the delivery room when our son is born, will be me." He seemed to think about it for a second. "Unless you'd like your sisters to be there. That of course would be acceptable."

I blinked. "We don't know for sure that it's a boy."

"Consider what I told you about my lineage. Odds are that it *is* a boy."

"Well, I—"

"Max Dubois can go have his own child," Philippe declared. "He won't be hovering around mine."

"Whoa," I said. "You are jealous."

"Not jealous, no," he said. "Possessive? *Absolument*."

I scrunched one eye up in consideration. "Huh? That sounded like you said—"

"Absolutely," he over pronounced.

"Oh, *absolument*," I tried out the French word for myself. "Absolutely?"

"*Oui*—yes." He tossed up his hands. "You need to learn French."

"And you need to stop tossing out random French words all the time! It's totally confusing."

Philippe shook his head and began to mutter, once again, in French. While I had no idea what he was saying, the aggravated tone was still crystal clear.

"Muttering in French is worse." I pointed out.

"How very inconsiderate of me, not to speak in *Anglais*," he snapped.

"Now you're being an asshole, Philippe." Fed up, I stood. "This whole throwing French words and phrases at me when you're angry is condescending and rude!"

"Gabriella," he said slowly and deliberately. "For your information, I was born and raised in France. English is *not* my first language."

"Well it is mine!" I knew he was mad, but I stomped over and got up in his face anyway. "How in the hell am I supposed to have a decent argument with someone who is speaking a foreign language!"

"You appear to be doing fine, *harpie*," he said sarcastically.

I narrowed my eyes. "Did you call me a harpy?"

"No, I called you a hell-cat," Philippe corrected.

Offended, I poked him in the chest. "Listen, buddy."

"Buddy?" He scowled down in my face, looming over me. "I am not your *friend*, Gabriella."

"There's a news flash!" I planted my hands on my hips. "What the hell are we to each other anyway?"

"We are lovers." Philippe tossed the words out as if he were daring me to argue.

"Lovers?" I scoffed at that. "A one-night stand three months ago, and a few kisses since then hardly qualifies us to be in the 'lovers' category, Marquette."

"Would you like me to rectify that situation?" he asked, softly.

"Rectify?" I growled in frustration and spun away from him. "Who talks like that anymore? You goddamn, arrogant, possessive, gorgeous Frenchman..."

I felt his hand on my arm a second before he spun me around and pulled me back to him. "And you are a stubborn, aggravating, beautiful woman," he said.

I landed with a slight thump against his chest. "I'm not beautiful," I said automatically.

"Yes you are." Philippe wrapped his arms around me. "And you called me gorgeous while you were ranting."

"No, I called you arrogant and possessive..." I trailed off as he leaned down, and his mouth hovered above mine. Our eyes locked, and I found myself unable to look away or even think coherently. I quivered, and his smile was slow and triumphant.

"*Ma belle*." He brushed a soft kiss across my lips.

My hormones erupted. "Philippe," I pleaded. "Don't distract me while we're arguing."

He tipped me back slightly and kissed me again. "Are we still arguing, *harpie*?

I wrapped my arms around his waist. "I think so." I lifted my mouth to his and kissed him back. It was humbling to realize that arguing with him had turned me on. *Had I become so cliché?* I thought. *And hold up...wasn't that a French expression?*

Our kiss became more intense and I stopped thinking altogether. Our tongues dueled and I ran my hands over his back and down and around to his butt.

"Gabriella," he asked, coming up for air. "Are you feeling well?"

I was having some trouble processing his question. "I'm fine." I managed between kisses.

"Good," he said. "Then I can do what I've been wanting to for the past month." He kissed along the side of my neck. "*Je te veux nue dans mon lit*," he whispered in my ear.

"Huh?" I said. "What's that mean?"

"Let me show you," he murmured, and picked me straight up off the floor. I twined my arms around his neck and held on. I gave his earlobe a nip as he walked across the room. Philippe nudged open another door with his hip and carried me into his bedroom.

CHAPTER NINE

Je te veux nue dans mon lit, translated to: 'I want you naked in my bed'.

I woke up—wait for it—naked, in his bed the next morning, and our second night together had been as good as the first. Better maybe. Philippe had been intense, yet still a considerate lover. I'd worried what he would think when he saw my baby bump, and if anything, it seemed to only turn him on more.

There was no doubt in my mind that the man wanted me sexually, but how he felt about me emotionally, I wasn't sure. *We had time,* I reminded myself. *Plenty of time to work things out.*

I peeked over at Philippe. He was out cold, one arm flung to his side. The morning sun was starting to illuminate the room, and I was tempted to cuddle closer, but nature called.

Slowly, I eased out from under the covers, slipped my midi dress over my head and headed for the bathroom. I was on my way back when I passed his dresser. Hanging from its ribbons and dangling from the mirror, like a trophy, was the midnight blue mask I'd worn to the party back in June.

My heart gave one hard lurch in my chest. Checking to ensure he was still sleeping, I stood on my tiptoes and eased it down. I stared at the mask in my hands with a combination of hope and fear. *He'd saved it. Maybe it was an important memento to him?* I wondered. *Or had he kept the mask because he was spellbound?*

As silently as possible, I slipped from the bedroom and headed back to the tower room. A few lamps were still on, and the morning sun filtered softly through the open windows. There was a slight nip in the September air, and I shivered. However, my hands were shaking with anxiety, not from the cool temperatures, as I crossed to the side table he used as a bar.

Determinedly, I grabbed a bottle of vodka and sprinkled some across the fabric mask. I set the bottle down and went to the fireplace. I would have to work fast, and luckily for me kindling was set in preparation for a fire. I spotted a box of matches on the mantle and steeled myself for what I had to do.

I knelt at the hearth, shook my hair back, and placed the mask on top of the kindling. Opening the box of matches, I began to reinforce the spell I'd started in my gardens the night before.

"By the powers of fire." I lit the match and set the flame to the edge of the mask. "By earth, air, and water; goddess hear the call of your daughter." I held the match in place and continued with the verse. "Fire burn and do what's right, speed my magick in it's flight. A love conjured is a false love and so it must burn away; any magick that influenced Philippe Marquette is ended this day."

A bright blue flame engulfed the mask, and I dropped the spent match. As I watched, the fabric covering it began to burn, almost unnaturally fast. Flames shot up and the kindling began to snap as the fire grew stronger. Determined to finish this, I held my hands out to the fire, adding my own personal power to the spell. I had to be sure to remove any remnants of magickal influence that might still linger on Philippe.

"Under my spell no more, your heart is now free," I chanted. "By all the power of three times three."

A rush of wind came whistling toward the manor, and the curtains billowed inwards as a strong breeze pushed into the room. The light bulbs in the lamps became suddenly bright, and their filaments all burst with loud pops of sounds.

I squeaked in surprise, pushing back from the hearth. Instinct had me glancing up just in time to see the framed portrait of Pierre Michel Marquette slide down the wall. The painting landed with a thud on the wide mantle. A second later, the burning mask broke in half with a loud crack, sending sparks shooting out of the fireplace.

The spell had been broken. With what sounded like a woman's sigh, a puff of blue smoke drifted from what was left of the mask and rolled up the chimney.

Standing in the tower room, with only sunlight coming in through the windows, I made sure to finish up my magick. "As I will it, so mote it be," I said formally. With my closing words, the wind died and the curtains dropped back into place.

"What in the world was *that*?" Philippe's voice was ragged.

I spun and found Philippe standing in the doorway. His dark eyes were much too large in his face.

"Philippe," I said, resigned.

"What did you do?" he asked, standing there only in a pair of unsnapped jeans.

"Maybe you should sit down." I said, noting how pale he was. "You don't look good."

Philippe drug a shaky hand through his hair. But he did as I suggested and sat on the couch. "Was that magick?" he asked after a moment.

"Yes, it was." The fire was merely a normal one now, and I checked on the framed portrait. It seemed to be fine where it had landed on the mantle. The old painting was leaning against the wall, and the frame appeared to be undamaged. I squinted up at the face of Pierre Michel Marquette, and a chill slid down my spine. If I didn't know better, his expression seemed to have changed to one of disapproval. "I don't like you either, pal," I muttered to that smug face.

"What did you say?" Philippe asked.

"It was nothing." Slowly I sank down to the hearth, tucked my legs beneath me, and faced him.

"Gabriella, please explain yourself." Philippe's voice was a little shaky, but not angry.

I figured I'd better keep it simple as not to frighten him. "You walked in on me finishing up a spell."

"It's true." He leaned forward, resting his elbows on his knees. "*Tu es une femme sage—* you are a wise woman," he translated, before I could ask.

"Yes. I am." I nodded my head and watched him closely, trying to gauge his reaction.

"Why would you feel the need to do a spell in *my* house?"

His question was fair, but the tone had my hackles rising. I rested my hands in my lap and chose my words carefully. "I cast a spell a few months ago. A specific type of spell on myself, so I would be brave enough to tell Max how I felt about him."

"What has this to do with us?" Philippe asked impatiently.

"It has to do with us, because I cast a glamour. A spell that would make me be seen as confident, beautiful and bold."

"Yes?" His eyebrows were way up.

"I put that spell into the mask that I wore to the masquerade party."

Philippe seemed to hold his breath. "Go on."

"Glamour spells can be tricky, and the spell didn't manifest quite as I'd expected," I said. "Max was charmed by a mystery woman, but the moment he found out it was me behind the mask—"

"He rebuffed you," Philippe finished my sentence. "I remember. I saw the whole thing."

"That's correct." I nodded. "The glamour didn't turn out like I'd hoped, and at that point I ran into you..."

"And?" Philippe demanded.

"And I've been worried that the spell might have accidentally transferred somehow. Creating an adverse effect on you."

"You're saying that you spelled me?" Philippe's tone was incredulous.

"Not deliberately." I swallowed past the fear in my throat. "The glamour was intended to help *me* to feel beautiful and desirable. *Not* to sway anyone's emotion's or to manipulate their attraction to me."

"*Ma belle,* I don't understand the exact workings of all this," Philippe said, sounding almost reasonable. "When you and I ran into each other after Max left, you weren't wearing the mask."

"I know that. But I did put the mask back on, and we danced together afterwards. We kissed later, and we ended up..." I trailed off and my eyes were drawn to the spot where we'd made love on the carpet.

"Gabriella, I think you might be overreacting."

My head snapped up. "No, I'm not. I've never in my life had sex with someone I'd literally only met a few hours before."

Philippe frowned. "And now you are unhappy with the way things turned out?"

"No, I'm not unhappy!" I shouted. Catching myself, I lowered my voice. "Let me be plain. I was afraid that the magick may have manipulated you into having sex with me, when you normally wouldn't have given me a second glance."

He response was to stare at me, unblinking.

"Philippe," I tried to make him understand. "There's no *logical* reason for someone like you to be attracted to me. You're a gorgeous Frenchman, with an impressive heritage, and I'm a regular chick who lives in a small town in Illinois. I work at home, have a smart mouth, and am pretty damn average looking."

"Gabriella," he tried again, but I ruthlessly cut him off.

"I know how this all seems. It appears calculating and manipulative, and I can't believe you haven't thrown me out of your home."

There, the truth was out. I didn't feel any better for telling him. In fact, all I wanted to do was cry.

"Do you believe that all of this..." He made a circling motion with one hand. "What we have found together, and the child, is because of a spell?"

"I've been trying to tell you that I'm concerned that it *might* have been. When I saw the mask in your room this morning, I destroyed it." I gestured to the fireplace. "I wanted to make damn sure that the glamour is broken once and for all."

He looked from the kindling that was burning out and back to me. "Meaning what, exactly?"

"That you are free of me," I said, bluntly. "Your will is your own."

Philippe scoffed and rose to his feet.

"Please listen to me!" I said. "If your kindness over the past few weeks, and us being together now, is because I manipulated your emotions with magick..." My voice broke. "Then I don't deserve to be with you."

Philippe walked over. He stopped in front of me, staring down as I sat on the hearth. "You honestly think I am only with you because of a spell?"

I stood to face him, and my knees began to tremble. "I don't know," I whispered as he continued to look into my eyes. "How do you feel now, knowing everything?"

He slipped a hand into my hair and tipped my face up to his. "Come back to bed, Gabriella." His voice was gentle and persuasive.

Even as my heart soared in hope, I told myself to be cautious. "You say that like you have...do you still have strong feelings for me?"

"Let me show you, *ma belle*." He kissed my forehead. "Your worries are for nothing."

"Wait." I rested a hand against his chest. "Maybe we need to give this some time. I should probably be away from you for a while and make sure the magick has run its course. After that, *then* you can decide how you feel about everything."

"I am fine." He tugged me up on my toes. "Unless it is *you* who needs to find an excuse to decide what your feelings truly are."

Now I was confused. "What are you talking

about?"

"Max," he said. "You think you can simply wait for him to love you, now that the spell is broken."

"No I don't," I answered him truthfully. "Besides, Max doesn't love me like that, Philippe. He is head over heels in love with Nicole."

Philippe tightened his grip in my hair. "Know this, Gabriella. For me, when I saw you that night it was *le coup de foudre*."

"I don't know what that means," I whispered.

"Yes, I know you don't." Philippe loosened his grip in my hair, and gently cupped the back of my head with both of his hands. He drew me to him, and his kiss was devastating. It was soft, sexy and intense. He lingered over it, and finally he let me go.

"Philippe, I...I..." I stumbled back from him. *I think I've fallen in love you,* I wanted to say. But I remained silent. Saying those words would be the ultimate in manipulation, especially now, and I couldn't do that to him.

"I'll take you home," he said gently. "It seems we both have a great deal to think about."

***

It wasn't exactly the walk of shame, but as I padded barefoot up the garden path to the backdoor of the farmhouse it sort of felt like it. My mind on everything that I'd confessed to Philippe, I didn't notice Drusilla weeding the faery garden until she spoke.

"Good morning!"

"Ack!" I jumped about a foot straight up in the air.

"Where's your shoes, Cinderella?" she asked.

"Dru." I pressed my hands to my heart. "You scared the shit out of me."

She tipped back the brim of her khaki ball cap. "For a woman who was out all night, you don't look very happy."

I slipped my hands in the pockets of my dress. "It's complicated."

"Step into my office." Dru pointed to the wooden bench.

I sighed and shuffled over to the bench. As I took a seat, Dru peeled her work gloves off, deliberately set them aside, and shifted from the kneeling position she'd been in to cross-legged on the grass. The tortoiseshell feline she'd named Mama Cat stepped out of the perennial bed and made herself at home on Dru's lap.

"Now," she began, "you're probably wondering why I asked you here today."

My lips twitched. "Smart ass."

"It was only a few months ago, that you sat me down and gave me some excellent advice about how sometimes, someone unexpected comes along..."

"Aw, hell, Dru," I said, resigning myself that I wouldn't be getting breakfast anytime soon.

Her robin's egg blue eyes were direct as she studied me. "Ella, I love you, but you have to be one of the most stubborn people I've ever met in my life."

"I'm a Capricorn," I shot back. "It's one of the perks."

The back screen opened with a creak, then it slapped shut. "Morning!" Cammy called out. She strolled down the back steps with a mug in one hand and a bottle of juice in the other.

I braced myself. Apparently the daughters of

Midnight had been lying in wait. Cammy sat herself right next to me. She greeted me with a kiss on my cheek. "Hi ya, Mum." She handed me a bottle of apple juice.

"Thanks." I twisted the top off the bottle and took a swig.

"Rough night?" Cammy asked, resting her hand on my arm. It only took her a second. "You found the mask, didn't you?"

There would have been a time that I would've found her reading my thoughts annoying. Right now it only helped me cut to the chase. "I did."

"Did you destroy it?" Drusilla asked.

I opened my mouth to ask how she knew, but Cammy piped up. "I told her about the situation, late last night."

I nodded. "I found the mask early this morning, and burned it in the fireplace at the mansion, while I thought that Philippe was sleeping."

"Did you go full bell, book and candle on it?" Cammy asked.

"Oh yeah." I took another sip of juice. "I also worked some of the ritual from last night into it, to cover my bases. The spell is definitely broken. I've rarely seen magick manifest on the physical plane like this one did. The problem is that Philippe walked in, and...he saw it all too."

"Uh-oh," Dru said.

"How'd he take it?" Cammy wanted to know.

I took a deep breath and filled my sisters in. I told them how the magick had behaved, Philippe's reaction to my confession, *and* my request that we give things some time to make sure the magick had run its course. "He seemed to take witnessing the magick better than our conversation afterwards," I said.

"How so?" Dru wanted to know.

"He overheard Max and I talking yesterday." I cringed remembering it. "Philippe thinks I still have feelings for Max."

"Do you?" Cammy asked, straight out.

"Romantic feelings?" I shook my head. "No, I don't. What I feel for Philippe makes me realize..." I trailed off with a sigh. "It doesn't matter now."

Dru patted my knee. "When you passed out the morning you came to tell us about the baby, Philippe was pretty worried."

"Worried about the baby." I said as the cat came over to give my bare toes a sniff. "Not me personally."

"He has been bringing you apples and fudgesicles, and taking you for walks," Cammy pointed out.

"That's because he wants me to be healthy, that way the baby will be healthy. It doesn't take a genius to figure that out."

"That doesn't explain him bringing you flowers for the last several weeks, Einstein." Cammy rolled her eyes.

"But how would I know if any of this—his behavior, I mean—is genuine or not?" I started to cry, and it embarrassed the crap out of me. "Stupid pregnancy hormones!"

"Oh, honey," Dru rose up to her knees and gave me a hug. "Have you considered that perhaps Philippe truly does love you?"

"No." I sniffled. "I'm afraid to let myself hope that his feelings are genuine."

"Has he talked about his feelings?" Dru asked, wiping my tears herself.

I started to laugh. "How would I know? He tends to speak in French when we—" I cut myself off.

"Oh don't leave me hanging!" Cammy laughed. "What does he say? I bet it sounds *hot*! Is it hot?"

"I have no idea what he's saying in the...er...heat of the moment," I admitted. "Half the time I think he does that on purpose. I'm at a real disadvantage."

"Well that seems fair," Dru said, reasonably.

"We should get you a French dictionary," Cammy suggested.

"That wouldn't do me a hell of a lot of good." I frowned at Cammy. "I don't even know how to spell the words he's pronouncing."

Dru and Cammy burst out laughing, and I sucked in a sharp breath. Suddenly, I felt the strangest flutter inside my abdomen. *Was that the baby?* I pressed both hands to my bump and held my breath. A few seconds later, I felt it again.

"Ella?" Dru jumped to her feet. "What is it?"

"I felt the baby move." I exhaled and began to smile. "The weirdest little fluttering."

"Really?" Cammy pressed a gentle hand to

my bump. "I wanna feel."

I laid my hand over hers. "I don't think he performs on command."

Cammy narrowed her eyes. "You said, *he*. Care to share with the rest of the class?"

"Philippe told me that there hasn't been a female born into the Marquette line in five generations—" I stopped as I felt it again.

Cammy bounced on the wooden bench. "Hey, I felt that!" She snatched Dru's hand and placed it where hers had been.

Apparently the baby was in the mood to perform for his aunts because I felt an even stronger flutter. I sat with my sisters and vowed to myself to hold onto this memory, no matter what. It was such a wonderful moment.

Dru began to cry happy tears. "Oh that's the best magick, right there. Hi, little guy."

"I still say it's a girl," Cammy argued.

Dru laughed at that. "Maybe. But to be on the safe side, Ella, you'd better start considering boys names."

"I started kicking around the name Daniel," I said. "After our dad." My statement had both of my sisters falling silent.

"You'd name the baby after daddy?" Cammy said.

"I was thinking about it." Now however I was worried, seeing the shocked expressions on their faces.

"I think that's absolutely perfect," Dru said, brushing away a tear.

CHAPTER TEN

I was soon to learn the difference between Philippe being charming, flirty and attentive and him being simply polite and kind. When my next doctor appointment came around a few days after our big talk, Philippe had accompanied me. He was caring, courteous and yet...distant. Gone was the charming Frenchman who'd kissed me, held my hand, and brought me flowers and fudgesicles.

In his place was a more formal and restrained Philippe, and by the time he'd dropped me off back at the farmhouse, I was torn between anger and disappointment. Clearly all that romantic behavior from the past month *had* been because of the spell.

I told myself I was damn lucky that the father

of my child was interested at all and tried to suck it up. But I'd be lying if I said it didn't hurt like hell.

I threw myself into staying busy with my web design. Working from Nicole's copious notes, I made the changes to Max's website for the autumn season and was relieved when I received a commission for cover art on an urban fantasy novel. I bunkered down in my office in the attic for the next several days, only coming out for the basic necessities. Bathroom breaks, eating meals, and tumbling back into bed to sleep.

Five days passed before I heard from him again. When I finally got a text from Philippe I snatched my phone off the nightstand so fast it was embarrassing. My heart soared with hope, but ultimately, I was disappointed. He wasn't texting his love, instead he'd politely informed me that he would be out of town for a week or so. After reading the brief message with a pounding heart, I wondered how to answer.

"What should I text back?" I asked myself. "'Sorry that I spelled you, you gorgeous Frenchman'. Or maybe I could send, 'I miss you'?" After a long moment I sent back a simple *OK* in reply. With a disappointed sigh, I rolled over on my back. Shadow the cat took that as an invitation and walked across my chest with a feline mutter.

"He says he's going out of town, Shadow." I sniffled a bit. "Probably going to put an ocean between us. He'll hide away in France to make sure the spell has faded...and that, will be that."

My phone vibrated. Philippe had sent me another message: *Take care of yourself,* he'd sent. After reading it, I dropped the phone on the bed.

"Meow." Shadow sat on my ribs.

"He did tell me to take care." I rubbed my hand over the cat's head. "Which is nice, I suppose. But it kind of seems like a kiss off after the past month... not that I don't deserve it." I groaned and flung my arm over my eyes. "Karma, thou art a heartless bitch."

My bedroom door was shoved open and it bounced off the wall. "Rise and shine!" Drusilla's voice was perky enough that I thought about throwing something at her.

"Go away." I pulled a pillow over my face,

and Shadow scrambled off the bed.

The pillow was yanked away. "Gabriella Lynn Midnight," Dru practically sang. "It's time to get up."

I scowled. "I don't wanna."

"Brooke and I are going to the garden center this morning to get some cornstalks and mums, to decorate for the autumn equinox."

"Hooray," I said, sourly.

"You're coming with us." Dru sat on the edge of the bed, wearing a bright orange shirt, jeans and sturdy boots.

"Shouldn't Brooke be in school?"

"It's Saturday, Ella."

"It is?" I had completely lost track of the days while I was working...and feeling sorry for myself.

"Come on, be a sport. Go hit the showers and I'll make you French toast for breakfast before we go."

"Don't say French," I muttered.

"Okay, sure thing." Dru smiled as if I was handing her roses instead of thorns. "Bowl of cereal it is."

"I don't like you in the morning," I said,

climbing out of bed.

Dru's laughter followed me as I shuffled across the hall and slammed the bathroom door. Her knuckles made a business-like rap on the closed door. "You've got thirty minutes to clean yourself up and eat," she said. "Then we ride."

Twenty-nine minutes later I sat at the kitchen table, lacing up my chucks. I was wearing my maternity jeans for the first time. At fourteen weeks, I didn't have a choice anymore. I had tossed on a clingy, white V-neck pullover, tugged it down over my hips and pulled my hair back with a headband.

"You girls be sure and pick me out some nice mums while you're at the nursery," Gran said, sipping her tea.

"What color did you want, Gran?" I asked.

She thought it over. "Orange, and white, mostly white; maybe some gold."

I stood and shrugged on my denim jacket. "White? I've never seen you plant white mums before."

Gran smiled. "A dozen white mums for truth and fidelity. I have a feeling we're going to need them."

I didn't have time to argue, Dru was hot to get to the nursery. I grabbed my bag and followed her out to the family's old pickup truck.

We picked up Brooke who was chattering a mile a minute. She sat between the two of us in the cab, and her good mood was infectious. By the time we arrived at the garden center, I was in a much better frame of mind. I eased down from the truck, and while Brooke went to nab a cart I checked out the fall display Max had set up.

It was different this year. Slicker almost. I had to approve of the changes, even as I wondered who had done the displays. While Brooke ran around exclaiming over the hay bales made into a maze and the cornstalks on display, I took the cart and tagged along behind Drusilla.

She went straight to where the mums were all arranged in long rows on the far side of the parking lot. My sister began to select the mums whose blooms were barely showing any color, exactly as Gran had taught us.

"Where are the orange ones?" I asked her.

"This section here," she said.

"How can you tell?" I laughed. "You didn't even check the plant tags."

"You can identify the orange variety by the shape of the leaves." Dru held up a few pots and placed them both on the cart.

Brooke came skipping over. "How many white chrysanthemums does Gran want, again?" she asked.

"A dozen," I told her, smiling at how she'd started referring to our grandmother as *Gran*.

"I'm going to get another cart!" Brooke took off at a dead run.

By the time we'd selected all the mums, and bundles of cornstalks, we made our way to the small house Max used as a storefront. I strolled in and came to a complete stop. Nicole Craig was standing at the front counter, dressed in pressed khakis, a yellow garden center polo shirt and a light denim jacket. Gone was the old cash register, and she was efficiently ringing up customers on a tablet attached to a stand.

As quick as the brunette was working, I guess she'd finally drug Max into the twenty-first century and had updated his checkout system to a more efficient one.

"Hello!" Dru called out cheerfully.

Nicole waved at us, and with an effort, I stopped staring. The last thing I would have ever expected was for Miss Fashionista to be wearing sturdy work clothes and, *holy crap!* Tennis shoes.

I surveyed the subtle changes to the store area as Dru and Brooke started checking out. When a familiar hand dropped on my shoulder I turned to find Max. "Hi," I said. "Did you take on a new employee?" I tipped my head toward Nicole.

Max's grin was lighting fast. "Isn't she great? Nicole insisted on helping out on the weekends."

"That's nice," I said, and tried to make sure I sounded like I meant it. He was obviously love-struck.

Max looked down at my mid section. "Wow! All of the sudden, you're showing."

I almost flinched at the comment but reminded myself that I was going to have to get used to that reaction from people. I was definitely showing now, and folks were bound to talk. Deliberately, I shrugged. "It's only because I'm not wearing a loose dress that you're noticing it more."

"You look better these days." He gave my shoulder a squeeze. "How is everything going?"

"I'm fine."

"Is Marquette treating you okay?" Max wanted to know.

I was saved from answering him, thanks to Nicole. "Max," she called. "Would you load up the cornstalk bundles into Drusilla's truck for her?"

While Brooke and Dru followed Max outside, there was a sudden lull in the customers, and I found myself standing with only Nicole.

"Finally," she said, walking over, all smiles. "I've been wanting a chance to speak to you alone."

My shoulders stiffened automatically. Nicole dipped her hands in her pockets and did something I'd never seen her do before. She shuffled her feet.

"What's up?" I tried to sound casual.

"You make me nervous," she admitted. "Max sets such store by you, and I worry that you hate me…" She stopped and blew out a breath. "It makes me talk too much, and way too fast."

"I don't hate you," I said, eyeballing the pretty brunette.

"You don't like me very much either." Her lips twisted over into a sort of half-smile.

"I—" I hesitated, choosing my words with care. "Max was deeply hurt when you broke off your engagement a year and a half ago."

"Yes, I know." Nicole's eyes were bright with unshed tears. "It was the stupidest thing I've ever done. I panicked at the thought of getting married, the fuss of a big wedding, you see. I'm not close to most of my family, and with no support, I was overwhelmed."

"Knowing Max as well as I do," I said, "I'm guessing he was all 'full steam ahead' with a big, traditional wedding, and was completely clueless to you being that frightened."

Nicole blinked. "Yes, that's it exactly."

"You should have been honest and spoken to him about your fears, Nicole, instead of calling it off and running away." I heard my own words and internally cringed at the irony of it all.

"You are absolutely right." She nodded.

"Well..." I shuffled my own feet. "He's really happy," I said. "Happier than I've seen him in years, and that's because you are back in his life."

Her eyes began to fill, and tears spilled over. "I can't tell you how pleased I am to hear you say that." Her tone was sincere, and it made me want to try harder to be kind.

"I'm sorry for snapping at you, the day of the meeting," I said. "I was feeling pretty awful and well...*I* was nervous and unsure about everything myself."

"I completely understand." Nicole opened her mouth as if to say more, and stopped.

"Is there something else on your mind?"

Nicole checked over her shoulder to make sure we were still alone. "Max asked me to marry him again, and I said *yes*." She pulled her left hand out of her pocket and held it out.

"Congratulations," I said, automatically taking her hand. The ring was stunning. A large cushion cut diamond was set in a delicate art deco band made of rose gold. "That's some ring."

"I won't hurt him again, Gabriella," Nicole swore. She turned her fingers over and gripped my hand. "I accepted the proposal with the understanding that we'd make it official and get married quietly, and right away."

I slid my eyes up from the ring to meet her eyes. "I bet that made him happy." *Was I saying happy too much?*

I stood there in the garden center, holding the hand of the woman my best friend had proposed to. It was slightly awkward—considering everything that had happened—but maybe, things *had* ended up exactly as they should have.

Max walked back in, we both shifted to look at him, and a huge smile spread over his face when he noted how we were standing. "You told her," he said to Nicole.

I gave her hand a friendly squeeze. "She did," I said to him, and then I let go.

Nicole smiled and launched herself into his arms. They kissed, and Max dipped her back dramatically. Torn between tears and a smile, I went ahead and smiled. When I did, a piece of the hurt pride that I'd been carrying melted away.

"Congratulations, to you both," I said as Dru and Brooke came back in time to witness the big smooch.

"What's going on?" Brooke wanted to know, as Max set Nicole back on her feet.

"We're engaged!" Nicole flashed her diamond, and Dru pounced, making the appropriate oohing and aahing noises over the ring.

"It's sparkly," Brooke said.

"Did you ask her?" Max ran his hand over Nicole's shoulder.

"Ask me what?" I said, feeling confused.

"We were wondering, do you think your grandmother would perform the ceremony?" Max said.

Dru grinned. "Oh she'd love that. Gran hasn't presided over a wedding in a while, but I'm sure that she'd be honored."

"That's what we were hoping," Max admitted. "We don't want to wait."

"Do you have a venue?" Dru wanted to know.

"No not yet." Nicole's smile started to fade a little around the edges. "We were hoping for something small and intimate."

While they'd been talking, a picture of the gazebo in our gardens popped into my head. In my mind's eye it was decorated with swags of tulle, faery lights, and bunches of white potted chrysanthemums were grouped all around it. "How about the gazebo in our gardens?" I heard myself say.

"That's a wonderful idea," Dru said. She smiled at the couple. "What do you think?"

"In the gardens at your house?" Nicole's voice was soft and full of wonder.

"The gardens look great since Dru's been tending them, and we just bought a whole bunch of white mums," I said, thinking back to Gran's cryptic comment about 'needing them'. "It could be very pretty."

Max deferred to Nicole. "What do you think?"

"I love the idea," she breathed.

"Could we pull this off in a week?" Max asked Dru and me. "Say, next Sunday?"

"Next Sunday is a very auspicious day," Dru

said, smiling. "It's the harvest moon."

"How romantic," Nicole breathed. "Getting married during a full moon. Do you truly think —"

"You bet we could!" Dru said, enthusiastically.

While Dru and Nicole began brainstorming, Max took my hand and pulled me a few steps off to the side.

"There's something else I want to ask you," he said. "I was wondering if you would stand up for us."

"Wow." I managed, clearing my throat. "Well sure. I suppose someone has to be the best woman."

***

No wonder Nicole had run for the hills the first time Max had proposed. Max Dubois— with his easy charm and laid-back attitude— was actually a Groomzilla. I began to suspect him a few days after they'd announced their engagement, but now that we were less than twenty-four hours out from the ceremony...his

Groomzilla status had been one hundred percent confirmed.

Saturday morning Max arrived to drop off pumpkins and two dozen more potted white chrysanthemums. He literally had a clipboard with him, complete with a timeline. While Brooke and Dru loaded the fat pumpkins in the wheelbarrow, Max had started to second guess the arrangement of the hay bales, mini white pumpkins, and the potted mums that Drusilla already had in place around the gazebo—the very same arrangement that he'd approved the night before.

Garrett tried to distract him, it was clear that Dru's arrangements were great, but it didn't work. I tried to derail Groomzilla by asking about the new pumpkins he'd brought. "Hey Max," I said, picking up a large one. "I've never seen pumpkins that were this blue-gray color before. What are they called?"

"Jarrahdale blue," he said, taking it from me. "They are popular sellers these days and Nicole asked for them along with the white flowers."

"Oh. They're pretty." Cammy walked over to check them out. "I like the Cinderella pumpkin shape."

Max smiled at her, fussed at me about picking up anything heavy, and handed me my own personal copy of the timeline and his pages of notes. My eyes almost bugged out of my head as I read it over.

"Max," I muttered. "You need a hypo of thorazine."

"Isn't that an anti-psychotic?" Cammy asked under her breath.

"Yeah." I handed her the timeline. "I'd say he needs it."

"By the goddess," Cammy said after glancing at the papers and handing them back.

I discovered that a restaurant from Alton was bringing in a catered brunch for two dozen, and a local bakery was supplying fancy cupcakes. The bouquets were covered, as Drusilla had assured the groom—I meant the bride—that she could conjure up some soft and natural hand-tied bouquets of flowers, straight from our gardens. They'd managed to snag a photographer. Nicole's brother was going to walk her down the aisle and also act as a man of honor.

Cammy had volunteered to be in charge of the music, and damned if Max didn't have a list of songs for her to play during the ceremony and the after-party. I read through the rest of the notes and discovered that Garrett had donated a case of wine to the Sunday afternoon reception. Fortunately the weather forecast was clear and dry with high temperatures in the 60's. Max had the weather forecast printed out as well. Broken down by the hour.

Gran was all set to officiate, and I didn't bother to ask how they'd gotten a marriage license that fast. Someone in city hall had probably run screaming in fear at Max's determination to get married to Nicole as quickly as possible.

As I scanned his timeline, which included the arrival of the bride, the photographer, and Nicole's hair and makeup people...I sincerely hoped he'd at least allowed the woman to pick out her own wedding dress. I flipped a page to the front, noted that Nicole was currently getting a mani-pedi, and that Max was scheduled for a hair cut in an hour.

With the perfect excuse at my fingertips, I

folded the papers, stuck them in my back pocket and shooed Max off to his appointment. Once he had left, Gran came out and helped Dru rearrange the mums and new pumpkins into a prettier display than Max had insisted on trying to do himself.

Brooke couldn't stop snickering over Max. She and Cammy had already set up the rental chairs and were beginning to hang swags of tulle and faery lights inside the gazebo.

"Are all grooms like that?" Brooke wanted to know.

"No dear, they're not," Gran answered.

"Sheesh." Brooke rolled her eyes. "He was kind of crazy."

Cammy snorted out a laugh. "I never knew Max was this anal retentive. If it wasn't so hilarious, he'd be annoying."

Silently I had to agree. I rested my hands over my belly and wondered where Philippe was, and what he was doing.

Damn it, I really missed him. I wondered if he missed me.

***

I sat in my room the following morning with a basic face, wrapped in my robe, adding the last of the bobby pins to my hair. I'd braided the front of my hair loosely away from my face and wrapped the braids around the back of my head. It created a sort of crown effect, but also left the majority of my hair flowing over my shoulders.

I checked the back of my hair, satisfied with the casual, relaxed look, and turned my attention to the dress hanging from my closet door. I'd ordered the knee-length maternity dress on line. The lace dress featured a high waist, short sleeves and a scalloped hem. I'd paid extra to have it overnighted—but it was a nice dress. The color was a soft vintage rose, and I'd be able to wear it again throughout my pregnancy.

Nicole would arrive shortly, and the day's festivities would begin. I could hear Gran and Drusilla moving around, and Dru was calling for someone to bring her the hairspray.

A knock sounded on my door, and Cammy stuck her head in. Still in her pajamas, my sister was in full makeup. Her hair was artfully tousled, and almost completely pink these days.

"Want some help finishing your face?" she asked.

"I can do it," I said, adding some rose quartz drop earrings to my ears.

"Let the master work her mo-jo." She walked over cracking her knuckles and made me laugh.

"Don't make me look all gothic," I warned her.

I sat still while Cammy wielded her brushes. "So," she said, darkening my brows. "Have you heard from Philippe lately?"

"He left me a voice mail yesterday. I guess I missed his call while we were running around in the garden keeping Groomzilla calm."

Cammy selected a shadow palette in mauve and told me to shut my eyes. "Garrett said Philippe got back in town last night."

"He did?" I asked.

"Ella, don't frown," Cammy complained. "I can't do your eyes when you scrunch your face all up."

"I wasn't frowning," I said, making the effort to relax my face muscles. "Philippe didn't mention that he was actually back in Ames Crossing."

"What did he say, exactly?"

"That he was getting his family settled." I blew out a nervous breath. "It was sort of vague."

"Well you can talk to him after the ceremony," Cammy said, working the shadow across my lids.

"He's coming to the wedding?" My heart pounding, I went for a casual tone, and thought I pulled it off.

"Of course he is. I'm sure he's mostly attending to make sure that Max actually marries Nicole, and *not* you."

"That's not funny."

"It is from my perspective." Cammy patted my shoulder. "I'm all done."

I opened my eyes and checked my reflection. While the makeup was a tad heavier than I normally wore, it looked damn good. "Thanks, Cam. I can use all the armor I can get today."

Cammy sent me an arch look. "I figured as much. You look good, Ella."

"Amazing how that happens when you're not

dry heaving over the toilet every morning," I said, wryly.

"No seriously, you look great and it's going to drive Philippe crazy—no magick required." Cammy tipped her head, listening as a commotion sounded downstairs. "The bride is here. I'm heading down." Cammy darted out and I took a moment for myself.

I sank to the side of the bed and told myself to try and remain calm. I'd be seeing Philippe in a matter of hours, and I had no idea how it would go, or how he would react. With a sigh I rose to my feet and went downstairs to join the bride and my sisters.

CHAPTER ELEVEN

I stood in the gazebo next to my best friend as he waited for Nicole to walk down the aisle —or garden path as the case may be—and reminded myself to smile. Gran took her place as the officiant, and Cammy cued up the music. Pachelbel's Canon in D drifted sweetly across the gardens, and twenty guests all stood and turned to watch the bride, escorted by her brother, walk forward.

The bride was stunning in a lace dress of silvery gray. I was pleasantly surprised at her choice. Her A-line gown stopped just below the knees. With a simple crew neck and elbow length sleeves, it was perfect for an informal garden ceremony.

Her bridal bouquet was a mixture of fall

flowers, white mums and hydrangea blossoms that had morphed to a soft rose, surrounded by blue-green hosta foliage. Dru had softened the arrangement by also working in sprigs of lavender and feverfew. The message of the bouquet was: fidelity from the mums, devotion from the hydrangeas and hosta leaves, with luck and happiness from the lavender. The tiny daisy-like flowers of the feverfew symbolized both protection and loving affections. It was the perfect message for her bridal flowers.

Returning my attentions to Nicole—and not her flowers—I had to blink back a few sentimental tears, seeing the combination of nervous and thrilled expressions run across the bride's face.

Max was beaming in a dark blue suit and soft gray dress shirt, sans tie. Out of the corner of my eye I caught a glimpse of Philippe. He was in the second row behind Garrett, Drusilla and Brooke, and was standing next to a distinguished looking older gentleman with a mane of silver hair.

My heart gave one hard leap. I told myself not to be a coward and smiled directly at

Philippe. He inclined his head slightly in acknowledgement, then he gave his attention to the bride.

I tightened my grip on my own flowers, a smaller version of what the bride carried, and told myself to focus on my duties as Best Woman. The tiny tulle bag I held with Nicole's wedding band in it suddenly felt very heavy in my hand.

Nicole took her place beside Max, and her brother shifted to the bride's left.

"We are gathered here today..." Gran began the ceremony.

I found it wasn't hard at all to smile after the brief ceremony, I accepted Nicole's brother's arm and followed the bride and groom back down the aisle. I took my place at the end of the short receiving line, accepted a kiss on the cheek from Garrett, a hug from my sisters and Brooke. I spoke to a few acquaintances of Nicole's and suddenly found myself face to face with Philippe.

"Gabriella." He gave me a kiss on the cheek. "You look lovely."

"Thank you." I fought the urge to reach out

for him. We stared at each other for a couple of seconds, our eyes locked. Finally he stepped back, and the spell was broken.

"I'd like to introduce you to my *grand-père*, Henri Marquette," he said.

The elegant man I'd spotted at his side during the ceremony stepped up and took my hand. "I am happy to meet you at last, Gabriella."

Stunned at meeting his grandfather, I shook the man's hand. "Nice to meet you, sir." I finally managed to say.

More people were pressing forward in the line, and Philippe and his grandfather walked away and went to go speak to Garrett and Drusilla.

After the photos, the food, and the toasts, the bride and groom went to dance beneath the gazebo. I stood off to the side with my sisters as the couple danced to Etta James', 'At Last'. What would normally be an overused song seemed to fit the couple.

When their song was finished, Cammy called for the wedding party to join the couple on the dance floor, and John, Nicole's brother, took my arm. I allowed him to escort me out to dance with him. We made polite small talk while Frank Sinatra crooned, 'The Way You Look Tonight'. John switched to dance with Nicole, and I found myself partnered with Max.

Max was grinning as Nicole and John started to move around the gazebo in a formal foxtrot. They'd obviously had training.

"Wow," I said after a moment. "Your bride's got some moves."

Max grinned. "They used to compete when they were kids," he said.

People were cheering watching the siblings, and I couldn't help but smile. "That's very cool."

"She tried to teach me," Max said. He lifted my arm, encouraging me to duck under his in a sort of turn. It didn't go very well and we both laughed. "But, as you can see," he said, "I'm hopeless."

Other couples began to join in, and the gazebo became crowded quickly. The wedding might have been small, but the guests were ready to party. Seeing my chance for a discreet exit, I stepped back.

"I shouldn't monopolize the groom," I said, easing further back, and sure enough Max went to go find his bride.

While the music pumped out, I found a shady spot in the gardens and went to sit in an Adirondack chair. I kicked off the heels I'd worn. I rarely wore high heels, and my feet were screaming. I sat back with a sigh, resting my hands above my tummy.

Brooke came over with two cupcakes on a plate. "Brought you one." She sat beside me and passed one over.

"You are my favorite person today," I said, taking the cupcake.

"I've never been to wedding like this one," she said.

"Oh, you mean outdoors?" I said, peeling the paper from the treat. I took a bite with a happy hum.

"Well yeah, but it's pretty fancy and everything," Brooke said. "I never saw a bride that didn't wear white. But I like the blue and white pumpkins. It's pretty."

"Mm hmm," I said, enjoying the pumpkin spice cupcake. "All weddings are different.

Depends on the time of year and what the bride likes."

"What kind of dress do you think you'll wear when you and Philippe get married?" Brooke asked.

I swallowed wrong, dropped the cupcake in the grass, and began to cough.

Brooke thumped me on the back. "Are you okay?"

In an instant Philippe and his grandfather were at my side. "Gabriella!" Philippe's voice was concerned as he helped me to sit up straighter in the chair.

"I'm sorry!" Brooke said.

I waved her apology away. "I'm fine," I said. "Swallowed wrong."

Philippe handed me a bottle of water and I took a sip.

"I'll get you another cupcake." Brooke shot to her feet and raced across the yard.

"I'm fine," I repeated and patted my chest. "No big deal." Philippe stayed crouched at my side. "The baby is fine." I scooted forward to stand.

"Allow me," he said and pulled me to my

feet.

Henri stepped in smoothly. "No hovering, Philippe. She won't break."

I smiled. "Thank you, Mr. Marquette," I said, and meant it.

"Please *cherie*, call me Henri or *grand-père*." He gently patted my baby bump. "I am delighted to meet you, and my great-grandson."

I couldn't help but smile. There was something about the older man that I instantly liked. I took his hand and gave it a squeeze. "I've been feeling the baby move lately."

"You have?" Philippe asked. "When did this begin?"

"In the past couple of weeks," I said.

"I shouldn't have left you," Philippe scowled. "But you insisted that we take some time apart." he reminded me.

"Yes." I worked to keep my voice even. "I did it for your own good."

"Are you angry at me for doing as you asked?" Philippe asked.

"Maybe, now is not the best time..." I began, slightly flustered with his grandfather standing right there.

"Ah, I see." He folded his arms. "You are upset over Max and Nicole being married."

I sucked in an offended breath. "I was their best woman! It was my idea for them to get married under the gazebo. I'm *happy* for them both...and I can't believe you said that to me."

"*Are* you happy for them?" Philippe asked.

Henri broke in. "*Vous êtes un idiot, Philippe.*"

I tried not to laugh. "Did you just call him an idiot?" I asked Henri.

Henri pinned his grandson with a look and rattled off something in French. Whatever it was had Philippe's eyes narrowing. The older gentleman gave me an air kiss, which I didn't mind at all. "Excuse me," he said. "I am going to leave you two to speak privately, and go have a glass of wine."

I watched his grandfather move across the garden. He went straight to where Garrett was pouring wine for guests.

"Have you been thinking, *ma belle*, while we were apart?" Philippe said. "I certainly have been."

"Yes, I have. I missed you," I said honestly.

"And to answer your question from earlier, no, I'm not angry with you...it's just that you make me nervous."

"Come with me now," he said urgently. "To the house, we need to speak in private."

"Your grandfather is in town, wouldn't that be a little awkward?"

"He's not staying with me, he's at a hotel."

I studied his face. Philippe was putting off some very determined vibes. "It would have to be later," I said. "I promised to help clean up after the wedding."

"We need to speak about the future. Our future and the child's."

My stomach dropped. *Did he mean our future as a couple...or future as in custody arrangements?* In the background I spotted Brooke. "I'll see what I can do," I said. "Brooke is on her way over." I stepped back and flashed a smile at the girl.

"I got you another one!" Brooke smiled and passed me a new cupcake.

"You shouldn't eat all that sugar," Philippe announced, taking it from my hand. "It's not good for you or the baby."

His domineering attitude instantly annoyed me "Don't treat me like I'm not smart enough to take care of myself." I said, taking it back from him. "If I choose to eat a damn cupcake, then I will."

Philippe snatched the napkin Brooke had brought and in one quick move, he wiped the icing off the top of the cupcake. "Fine, but no one should have all that icing."

I stood there, torn between throwing the cupcake at him, laughing, and telling him off. I took a deliberate breath. "That sort of dominant, macho bullshit, is *not* attractive, Marquette."

"Ella, what's wrong?" Brooke glanced between me and Philippe. "Are you guys fighting?"

"It's okay, Brooke." I said, holding Philippe's gaze intentionally. "I suppose I wanted that cupcake more than I thought."

"I thought you two loved each other," Brooke said. "I mean, you're having a baby and everything."

"I do love her," Philippe said. "However, Gabriella is stubborn, and she doesn't always listen to reason."

Philippe's words had my mouth dropping open in shock.

"Brooke," Philippe continued as if nothing out of the ordinary had happened. "Why don't you get Gabriella some fruit salad instead?"

"Sure." the girl stood, studying us suspiciously. "I could do that. But no fighting while I'm gone," Brooke said seriously. "I mean it."

"But of course." Philippe gave her a mock salute and Brooke went scampering over to the buffet table.

The minute she was out of earshot I turned on Philippe. "I can't believe you—" The rest of my sentence was cut off when he grasped my arms, pulled me up to my toes, and kissed me soundly. Right in the middle of the wedding reception. In front of my family, his grandfather, and everyone else.

He lifted his mouth from mine. While I sputtered, he stood there and grinned. "Finally," he said. "I have found a way to shut you up."

"I'm sorely tempted to kick you in the balls," I said under my breath.

"Is that your idea of foreplay, *harpie*?" he said, grinning.

"Don't call me a hell-cat." I narrowed my eyes in suspicion. "What are you playing at, Philippe?"

Practically nose-to-nose with each other, he stared down into my eyes. "I am not playing at all."

"Then what—" I began.

"*Je t'aime*," he said softly.

Those words rocked me to the soles of my feet. And I knew exactly what they meant. *I love you.* The fact that he'd made that declaration in French made it more devastating somehow.

"Philippe, I—"

"I thought you should know," Philippe said. He let me go and I stepped back.

"I got you a bowl of strawberries!" Brooke announced cheerfully.

"Thanks sweetie," I answered automatically, but didn't take my eyes of Philippe.

"Tonight, Gabriella." His words made my stomach churn with anxiety. "We have many things to discuss."

I nodded to him. "If you'll excuse us, Philippe." My mind reeling, I walked away with Brooke. I got through the rest of the reception because I stuck to Brooke's side like glue. It was probably a gutless move, but it was the best option I had.

Eventually we waved the newlyweds off, and I helped Gran and Cammy take any leftover food inside. Garrett and Drusilla began to break down the rental tables, and Cammy folded up all the chairs. Brooke carried in the wedding gifts and a big box that held all of the cards, and Gran made a comment about putting her feet up and ordering pizza for dinner.

Philippe and his grandfather had left at some point after the newlywed's departure, and I spent the clean-up time giving myself a firm lecture on remaining calm and not letting myself be maneuvered by a certain sexy Frenchman. He wanted to talk? Well by the goddess, so did I. Embarrassing me, kissing me in front of everyone...dropping that quiet *I love you* in French in the middle of my best friend's wedding reception?

Philippe Marquette was in for an earful. I

grabbed a stack of napkins and felt a quickening in my belly from the baby, and all my bravado crumbled as easily as the leftover paper napkins from the wedding reception.

I had more to think about than only myself. I laid my hand on my belly. "Don't you worry little guy," I said. "I'll straighten this mess out."

***

It had taken a few hours but eventually I was able to slip out. I changed into a casual black empire waist dress, added a denim jacket, and laced up my comfy sneakers. Taking my time, I slowly drove my car up to Notch Cliff and parked it in the empty parking lot by the winery shop.

The moon was rising, and as I climbed from the car I felt its pull more than ever. I glanced at the old house and saw movement in an upper window. At first I thought it was Philippe keeping watch, but my impression was that it was a female.

It gave me a bit of a fright, since that window was in the uninhabited section of the mansion. I made myself check again, but saw nothing. Instead of going to the house, I walked across the grass toward the cliffs. Neutral ground would be best for the talk we needed to have.

Perhaps it was the emotional influence of the moon, my rampaging pregnancy hormones, or maybe I was simply wiped out from all the upheaval in my life; but all my courage left me as I stood there. The wind coming off the cliffs above the river whipped my hair back, and I tossed my head, ignoring the tears that had started rolling down my face.

The full harvest moon had risen completely, illuminating the river valley. Standing under its light, I hugged my arms across my middle and thought back to a magickal night in early June when I'd recklessly changed my fate forever. I'd longed for adventure, a passionate lover, and a romance of my own, and I'd gotten it. All of it.

Knowing what I did now, I still wouldn't change anything. The glamour I'd cast had brought wonder, magick, and an amazing man into my life. He'd said that he loved me...but did he truly? I wasn't sure if Philippe even trusted me.

I felt him approaching before I heard him.

"Gabriella," he called my name.

I wiped my eyes, but didn't bother glancing over my shoulder. He eased up to stand beside me and we stood together looking over the river.

"Why are you crying?" he asked, gently.

"Oh, I don't know," I said, miserably. "Lots of reasons."

"Tell me," he said softly.

"I'm crying because things are a mess. Because I fell in love with a man that I accidentally ensorcelled."

"Ensorcelled?" He tilted his head to one side. "What does that word mean?"

I almost laughed. That was typically my line. "It means bewitched, enchanted, or lured."

"It's difficult to have a talk with someone who throws out words in a foreign language." His voice was dry and solemn.

I shifted to look at him and saw that he was giving me an arch look. His tie and suit coat were gone, but he was still wearing the shirt and dress slacks he'd worn to the wedding. I sighed. "It's a magickal term, Philippe, but it was spoken in English."

"Do you remember?" he said as we stood side by side. "I once said that when I saw you that night of the masquerade, for me it was *le coup de foudre*."

"Yes," I said, pushing the hair from my face. "Although, I still don't know what that means."

"*Le coup de foudre*," he said, "means, love at first sight."

I jolted. "It does?"

He took my hand. "You came walking across the grass in that blue gown, the moonlight in your hair, and my heart was lost."

"Because of the spell."

"The spell you were so worried about never had anything to do with my feelings for you." Philippe turned and faced me directly. "Do you know how I felt the day you came to tell me you were pregnant?"

"No, I don't."

"Relieved," Philippe admitted. "Happy and *relieved* that now I had a chance to court you properly."

"Nobody 'courts' anymore, Philippe," I said.

"Not in this day and age."

"Most people don't believe in magick either," he said. "Perhaps that is what is wrong with the world."

I found I had nothing to say to that. If I hadn't realized I'd loved him before, those words would have absolutely cinched it for me.

Philippe took my hand. "Now, as I was saying before you interrupted, I had planned to court you properly with the hope that you would come to love me as much as I already loved you."

I tried to blink the tears away, but they continued to fall.

He smiled. "When you insisted we have some time apart to let the magick run its course, I agreed, but only because you were upset."

"It was only fair," I said, blowing out an unsteady breath. "How do you feel now that you've had some time to think things over?"

He brought my hand to his lips and kissed the back of it. "Gabriella, my feelings are unchanged. I loved you then as I love you now."

"I've been pretty unhappy without you, these

last few weeks," I admitted. "Scared you didn't really love me for myself, and worrying over the baby's future."

"I do love you, exactly as you are. Now, no more worrying. Everything will be fine, you'll see." He pulled a small velvet box out of his pocket. "Marry me, Gabriella."

"Wait, what?" I yanked my hands back. "What are you doing?"

"I should think that would be obvious." He went down on one knee and opened the ring box himself.

I stood staring at the ring. It was a simple diamond solitaire in a golden band, and it was perfect. "Oh my goddess," I said.

"Say yes, Gabriella."

I wiped my eyes. "Philippe, if I accept that ring, you're *not* going to rush me to the altar."

He grinned up at me. "Oh yes I am."

"No, you're not," I said. "I think we should live together first. That's only sensible."

"Even now, you have to argue..." He rolled his eyes to the moon. "Are all wise women this stubborn?"

"No," I said, straight faced. "You just got

lucky with me."

"How long are you going to make me wait before we can be married?" He took the ring from the box and held it up.

"Let me put it to you this way," I said, holding out my left hand, "I'm not wearing a maternity dress to my own wedding."

Philippe chuckled and slid the ring on my finger. "*Je t'aime,* Gabriella," he said.

I stared at the ring on my finger for a moment. "Philippe." Sliding my hands under his jaw, I kissed him. "*Je t'aime.* I love you too."

Philippe leaned forward to press his cheek to my baby bump. I held him to me and felt the baby move. He gasped.

"Did you feel that?" I asked.

"*Oui*—yes." He said, and tears filled his eyes. "Yes, I did."

"I guess the baby approves," I said, laughing and crying at the same time.

"Three months after our son is born, is all the longer I am willing to wait." He kissed my belly. "How do you feel about the month of June?"

I ran my fingers through his hair. "June *is* traditional," I said, and laughed again when he jumped to his feet and wrapped me up in his arms. We kissed, and the magick between us was wonderful and real.

"You know..." he said between kisses. "I'm very fond of June nights."

"I'll bet you are," I managed to say when he let me up for air. "After all, the first time you and I—"

He cut me off with another passionate kiss.

"I was going to say danced, Philippe." I nipped his bottom lip. "The first time we *danced*."

He murmured some French phrase in my ear. I had no idea what he'd said, but before I could ask, he proceeded to show me. Right there, under the full harvest moon in the soft grass high on the cliffs.

Afterward, we lay together in the grass. "I think you might be right," I said happily. "June does sound like a perfect time to get married."

He pulled me over to lie on top of him. "Get used to saying that," he said.

"Saying what?" I teased him.

His hand cupped my bottom. "Get used to saying: 'Yes, you are right, Philippe'."

"No way." I dropped a kiss on his nose. "It'll go straight to your head."

***

At our next ultrasound appointment, the doctor was able to determine the gender of the baby. And it ended up that Philippe *was* wrong about one thing.

The baby was a girl.

Turn the page for a preview of Camilla's story, and the third book in the "Daughters Of Midnight" series: *Midnight Prophecy.*

Midnight Prophecy
Daughters Of Midnight, Book Three

If there's one thing I know, it's magick.

It was an integral part of me, and I'd felt the beat of its rhythm since I was a little girl. Instinctively I understood its workings, the why and the how. Sitting in the gardens beside my Gran, I was quietly and carefully taught the natural tools of the herbalist's trade. I came to revere the energies of nature. I understood the cycles of the moon, and the tides of all four seasons. I learned to respect the elements, and the enchantment of tree, flower, and herb.

The roses in the garden could inspire friendship and romance. Lavender was protective and used for cleansing. The oak tree encouraged prosperity and knowledge, while sage brought wisdom and longevity. All of these lessons and many more I soaked up and integrated into my own life. I accepted my place in the overall design of it all, and I embraced my destiny as a wielder of its power.

Centuries ago they'd have called me a Witch, and my fate would not have been kind. Today, the females in my family referred to themselves as wise women, and although the term was often used interchangeably with Witch, *wise woman* suited me.

I considered myself a modern practitioner of the old ways. And with that thought in mind, I decided to honor my family's heritage, combine it with the skills I'd learned in my Gran's kitchen and gardens, and start a business of my own.

It was an irresistible challenge for me. Combining the historic remedies, potions and lotions of the wise woman, and turning it into natural products for the modern consumer. I was thrilled at the opportunity to shake things up and do something different—my pink hair not withstanding.

I was feeling quite proud of myself. My business proposal had been accepted, and I'd worked hard to save the money required for a start-up. With a schedule in place, projected timeline and professional goals all mapped out, *Camilla's Lotions & Potions* was ready to launch.

As I loaded the last of my stock into the family's old pickup truck, I was excited to begin and looking forward to this new chapter in my life. I certainly wasn't looking for romance, nor had I ever expected to deal with prophecies and curses. They simply had no room in the personal agenda I had so carefully organized and cultivated.

However, fate is a tricky beast and sometimes it has other plans for you. Plans you never saw coming, no matter how wise you think you may be.

My name is Camilla Jane Midnight, and this is my story.

ABOUT THE AUTHOR

Ellen Dugan is the award-winning author of over twenty-eight books. Ellen's popular non-fiction titles have been translated into over twelve foreign languages. She branched out successfully into paranormal fiction in 2015 with her popular "Legacy Of Magick" series, and has been featured in USA TODAY'S HEA column. Ellen lives an enchanted life in Missouri. Please visit her website and blog:

www.ellendugan.com
www.ellendugan.blogspot.com

Made in the USA
Columbia, SC
07 June 2021

39329627R00130